Love's Face

> *"ARISE, MY DARLING, MY LOVELY ONE, AND COME WITH ME ..."*
>
> *THE BRIDEGROOM*

MARGARET MONTREUIL

LIVING WATERS
PUBLISHING

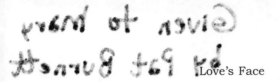

Love's Face

published by Living Waters Publishing

International Standard Book Number: 0-9659320-2-8

Most Scripture quotations are from the *New King James Version.*
Copyright
©1979, 1980, 1982, Thomas Nelson, Inc.

Printed in the United States of America

Living Waters Publishing
15590 Highland Avenue N.W.
Prior Lake, MN 55372
Toll-free: 888-950-2772 E-mail: Lvngwtrspb@aol.com

Publisher's Cataloging-in-Publication
(Provided by Quality Books, Inc.)

Montreuil, Margaret.
Love's face / Margaret Montreuil. -- 1st ed.
p. cm.
Includes bibliographical references.
ISBN: 0-9659320-2-8

1. Jesus Christ--Devotional literature. 2. Jesus Christ--
Meditations.   I. Title.

BT268.M66 1997   242
                        QBI97-40848

This book is dedicated to You, Jesus, most beloved Lord. Seven years ago You invited me to walk on water with You and write this. It's taken that long to learn and grow in You. Thanks for keeping me afloat. Thanks for everything You've so extravagantly shown me. Your timing is always perfect—as are all Your ways.

May this book be like the sweet anointing perfume of love with which Your devoted servant, Mary, poured on You about 2,000 years ago. With this book I anoint You first on Your head (You Yourself), then Your body (those who belong to You through faith), and Your feet (to help further this wonderful truth of Your love).

I ask that You bless this book and manifest Yourself and Your love intimately to every person who reads it. Enjoy this, Lord. I love and adore You.

Margaret

PREFACE

Something wonderful has dawned upon my life and, I believe, is dawning on many these days: God is passionately and intimately in love with us.

Love's Face—the face of God—cannot be seen physically but can be perceived spiritually; nor can God's love be fully understood intellectually. God is love. Only a heart can fully embrace Mystery. Our minds cannot. I believe mystical, spiritual love can be glimpsed through art, poetry, paradox, and symbolic images (like human love in marriage and practices in worship). God reveals Himself to one as Father, another as Friend, another as Good Shepherd, and the Captain of Hosts to another. The images we have of God are given to us by Him, to help us know Him. God reveals Himself to each heart the way He chooses. No one's revelation of God is better than another's. The image (revelation) of Jesus in this book is that of a soul's Lover—the Messianic Bridegroom and Divine Spouse of a soul.

I'd like you to know, revelation of the bridal, spousal love of Jesus took me joyfully by surprise. The great mystery Paul told us about of how "Christ loves the Church" is easier to think of in an abstract-kind-of-way than it is to intimately experience it ourselves. I did receive it, or should I say, that this great Mystery grasped hold of me! Pure grace! I often am filled with awe and wonder. It just seems too good to be true! I do not claim to understand it. I have come to see God as a great lover, even Love itself. Seeing His face, the longing of all believing hearts, is His sweet invitation to us. Perceiving God's countenance, through love, causes a delightful state of charity in the outward life, as well as the inward.

It is one thing to know about Jesus and quite another to know *Him*. This book is a book for the heart, written in a way that, hopefully, will bring you into true, intimate, encounters with Jesus. Experience it. It isn't a scholarly work. It is an invitation, if you will, to "see" Jesus' face, and to experience God's love. It's like a mini-faith journey, from the first recognition, to that of being in loving union with Jesus. It was prayerfully and worshipfully written for Him, about Him, and in Him—and for His bride.

A Word of Introduction

For many, bridal, spousal love with Jesus is a strange thought. Would God make the highest and sweetest expression of love for His creatures only, not to be enjoyed Himself? With God, there is neither male nor female; but "being in love with God" is certainly like that. If we can wrap our minds around the "concept" that God is like a male and the soul like a female it is easier to understand. All love is from God. God *is* that Love. All of His-story is a divine love story about This Tremendous Lover. If one would read the entire Bible from that perspective, how many times could you count God as acting like a "broken-hearted lover?" How often, and in how many ways, has Jesus been pursuing each and all of us? From the dawn of creation the Spirit has been wooing us, one by one.

By giving us Himself in the pledge and presence of the Holy Spirit, we enter into a divine love covenant (a divine engagement) with Him. He clothes us with wonderful grace, which is His unmitigated love. He redeemes us and gives us white garments, pure and spotless, to wear. God loves us as a bridegroom loves his bride.

Yahweh formed Israel into a people so that He could be in covenant relationship with them. Karen Mains, in her book, *Making Sunday Special*, explains that the Sabbath is a wedding ring God gave Israel. She says, ". . .the Hebrew word for 'sanctification' is the same as the word 'marriage'. . . . the Exodus passage becomes meaningful in relationship to the love motif, 'You shall keep My Sabbaths, for this is a sign between Me and you, through your generations, that you may know that I, the Lord, sanctify you (am married unto you).' The giving of the ring is the most important act of the entire Jewish wedding ceremony. The groom puts the ring on the index finger of the bride's right hand and recites: 'Behold you are consecrated to me with this ring according to the Law of Moses and Israel.'" She explains how this was a marital covenant God made with them.

God wanted a bride. Israel was set apart from all other nations because of this Sabbath covenant. Here we can begin to see a symbolic example of the mystery of Divine Romance.

God wanted to spend a sacred day, a kind of romantic get-away, each week with His faithful ones. Complete with a worshipful ritual, the evening of the Sabbath begins with a love feast with the family, complete with candles, fancy dishes and table cloth, prayers, lovingly prepared food, and rest. Historically, Israel, His beloved people, have been set apart—chosen and betrothed as His "own" people (though without faith in their Messiah Jesus they cannot understand or see His faithfulness to them). They will one day. Today, there is also a spiritual Israel—redeemed by God through a new covenant—the blood of the Jewish Messiah. We often gather around the Lord's Table and share in the bread and wine of Jesus' love covenant with us. And, observing the Sabbath as "His day" is a tradition we have kept over the centuries; as we "remember" Him we await our Bridegroom's physical return to Jerusalem.

The New Jerusalem, both physical as well as spiritual, is His bride. We (our hearts) are the spiritual New Jerusalem.

The Jewish wedding itself is a wonderful metaphor of Jesus marrying His Church. The groom first comes to the bride's home in an engagement ceremony, drinks a cup of wine as a pledge (this is where the vows of marriage become binding), and leaves gifts for the bride. He then returns home to His father's house and begins preparing living quarters for his bride and himself. When he is finished, the wedding procession travels to the bride's home, complete with musicians and friends, celebrating on the way. They come without warning, and surprise her and joyfully whisk her away. She must be ready to meet her bridegroom.

Jesus is the Great Bridegroom for whom we anxiously await. Until that day, our Bridegroom says to us: "Come. Arise, My darling, My lovely one, and come with Me." God calls us to Himself.

A Word of Instruction

Keep a prayer journal for the prayer exercises provided at the end of each chapter, dating your entries and recording your experiences during prayer. The prayer journal exercises are provided as a way to experience God. There is nothing that must be followed strictly but, rather, should be used to experiencially apply each chapter's theme. Feel free to modify or recreate your own prayer exercises from these if they don't work for you. On the other hand, it would be easier to skip the exercises and go on reading. Don't let yourself do that. If you have to go through the book slowly, for lack of time, go slowly. God is in no hurry and desires to spend time with you. Glorious joy will come from your times of personal face-to-face encounters with Him—during your prayer times. Personal transformation and spiritual growth in your faith journey comes from Him personally, not from cognitive learning alone. (One must receive God's love in order to love God.) Experiencing His presence in prayer is far better than reading about Him, or simply thinking about Him (good things to do); but it would be similar to being content to dream of being married someday and never bothering to meet, date, or get to know your future mate. Or, it's like coming to the front door of the Throne Room and then standing just outside, content to be near, but not before, God. He's interested in face to face. And that really is what this book is all about—seeing Love's Face and experiencing intimacy with Jesus.

TABLE OF CONTENTS

Chapter One

THE BRIDEGROOM COMES

A lone figure stood leaning against an old olive tree on the Mount of Olives. Jesus looked down at the splendid sight of His beloved Jerusalem, the holy city. Deep in prayer with His Father, He lingered there for a couple of hours. Together, they took in the awesome sight of this object of their passion— an ancient and living passion wrought with love and blood. This was His first visit to Jerusalem since He began His public ministry. Cool, gusty winds blew His hair and clothes about. Contemplative, He watched pilgrims pour through her gates for the week of Passover.

The ancient city had been built upon several foothills cradled within higher surrounding "mountains", one of which was the Mount of Olives, a long ridge of earthen wall that framed most of its eastern side. High golden walls of limestone blocks sprawled along these hilltops—up, down, and around—hemming in the entire city. Enormous gates stood like sentries at all her strategic entries. The city's panoramic view was magnificent from Jesus' position opposite and above the eastern gate. The Garden of Gethsemane was down the hill from Him at the foot of the mount.

When viewed from a higher, distant vantage point, the city looked golden as it reflected the brilliant sun, always an explosion of joy to Jewish pilgrims at the end of a long journey. In those days, Jews were already scattered in somewhat of a Diaspora, so many pilgrims traveled from near and distant countries to celebrate their holy feasts in the ancient City of Peace. Sudden awe would leap within their hearts when they'd mount some distant hilltop crest that would finally fill their eyesight with their longed-for, beautiful Jerusalem.

There has always been that mystical something about Jerusalem that draws and gathers God-seeking pilgrims to her. From the time of Abraham, who first proved his faith there, to the prophetic future when all the nations' leaders will stream to the City of the Great King during the Messianic Age, Jerusalem has been central to faith and worship. The Hebrew name for God is "written" in the geographic formations of the city. The very hills and valleys of Jerusalem spell His name. It can be plainly read from an aerial view.

Of course the Messiah loved her. How could He help but weep and ponder about all that Jerusalem meant?

The prophetic eastern gate He watched opened directly to the front of the majestic temple. Now facing Him, it stood stately, erect and tall. Its very architecture and design inspired faith in the Lord God of Israel. Here was housed God's *shekhinah*—His splendor, His presence—here, on earth, at this holy place. Here eternity and infinity met in time and space. God's presence was Jerusalem's glory! The temple was splendid, made with white marble and golden stone, with massive, artistically carved wooden doors. It was skirted and graced by surrounding wings, stately court systems and buildings—all ranked by rows of white marble columns.

The temple's Most Holy Place was the building's tallest part which seemed to wear a crown of glittering gold from engraved artwork that trimmed its pinnacle. Jerusalem was the Lord God of Israel's "Queen." That day in early spring, did she know she was dressed and adorned for her Bridegroom? This was His betrothed city, the symbol of His bride, Israel, and all those faithful to Him.

Enraptured by her beauty and pained by her ignorance, Jesus stood on the brink of the greatest drama of eternity. The great mystery of God's redemptive love would soon be revealed.

As little rivers of love trickled down His face, He brushed away the tears with His sleeve. He was filled with the sudden realization and excitement that the time was upon Him—the time for which He'd been so patient—the days of Jerusalem's visitation. He knelt down on the stony ground, bowed His shoulders humbly, His forehead to the ground. He surrendered Himself to His Father's whole and entire will—the divine plan of salvation, planned before His incarnation, even before the foundations of time. One with His Father, He renewed His vow to fully give Himself to, and for, their "Bride." He knew who He was. He knew what He must do.

Jesus arose and carefully picked His way down the steep slope, and joined the stream of other pilgrims moving towards the temple complex. His own pilgrimage had been the farthest of all to this meeting place. Alone in a crowd, He passed through the City of David and entered the temple area through the eastern gate. This was the gate the Messiah was prophesied to pass through in glory. But Jerusalem was unaware of the promised prophesies when Jesus, the long awaited Messiah, walked unobtrusively into His temple, unnoticed, quietly moving among His people. He paused before the inner gate which led into the Most Holy Place and watched worshipers handing their lambs to the priests for sacrifice. He gazed up at the tallest part of the temple, the Holy of Holies. Smiling, He thought about the day of redemption when He would pass through the true veil-of-separation which separated God from man.

The curtained veil-of-separation in this temple was like it. The high priest would bring the blood of the sacrificial offering through the massive veil of curtains and present it before God in the Most Holy Place, before God's presence. This brought forgiveness for the people's sins. Jesus, the promised Great High Priest, and spotless Lamb of God, would soon offer His own blood for the forgiveness of sins. To those who would believe in Him, His holy and righteous blood would bring just and eternal atonement, once and for all. No longer would there be that sin-driven separation. Jesus would build a new temple in a heavenly Jerusalem—within the hearts of His people on earth—and separation between them need be no more.

Jesus stood there, lost in thought, until somebody bumped into Him, a man from the edge of a pushing crowd streaming by. The temple area was getting busier by the minute. Jesus apologized to the man for blocking traffic flow and then turned away. He headed for the temple's side courts, and took in the sights, sounds, and smells. He delighted in the smell of the incense and smoke which joined and rose with the prayers and worship of the faithful. Jesus loved to be in the temple.

Eventually, He reached the court where He had agreed to meet several friends who had been disciples of John, The Immerser. They were His own disciples now. As He came into the makeshift marketplace that had been set up there for years, the contrast between the sacred and the chaotic made Him sick at heart; and the sights of profane spiritual abuse moved Him to anger.

There were fenced-in areas of sheep, goats, and cattle, and the smell was terrible. He saw dung piled against a column. Cages of doves and pigeons were stacked near the place where the priests blew the shofar which called the faithful to times of corporate prayer. It was noisy, congested, and dirty. Merchants yelled and peddled their wares to passersby. Moneychangers were cheating worshipers who needed temple currency to purchase animals. Because these animals were sold and then sacrificed for worship, it was an exorbitant profit-making business for many greedy religious leaders of the Sanhedrin. Faithful pilgrims had no choice but to buy their animals from them at inflated prices. It was a racket. The marketplace was brimming with injustice, foul sights and smells, and chaos— right within the temple courts of the Lord.

Now was the time! No longer would He simply walk past this abomination as He had before. Jesus met His friends at the agreed-upon archway. Spying ropes lying near an animal pen, He abruptly explained that He had something He needed to do right away. They watched Him pick up the ropes, sit down on a crate and fashion a whip. His hands worked skillfully fast while His eyes stole quick glances around and mentally planned His strategy of attack.

He stood when finished and quickly made His assault. His eyes flashed a holy fierceness. His knuckles were white as He tightly gripped the knotted handle of the crude whip. Merchants who challenged Him found themselves shoved aside. Sometimes using a foot or hip, He pushed over tables and stands while opening cages and pens. He drove away sheep and goats with the whip. The animals bleated loudly and ran wild in all directions with their owners chasing them in like manner. His enraged commands echoed throughout the courtyard as He worked, "Take these things away!" Dozens of fluttering doves and pigeons found freedom above the heads of their keepers. "Do not make My Father's house a house of merchandise! This is a house of prayer!" His movements were deliberate and swift, going from setup to setup. "How dare you turn My Father's house into a den of thieves!" He picked up money boxes and threw them; as they crashed, coins rolled in all directions. "You crooks! Get all these out of here!" Long tables filled with things flipped upside down when He discarded the rope and went to using both hands. None of the temple guards tried to stop Him. His raging righteousness prevailed upon all like stormy weather over a landscape, and they had nothing to do but get out of His way.

Futile, empty, and polluted religiosity needed the whip of His jealous love. The heart of God was crying out against religious-looking wolves who preyed on those with sincere devotion. He was upset by their darkened understanding that led them to create this despicable marketplace. How He longed for them to know and enjoy what true worship and communion with God could mean—prayer and relationship. Not this! God, in Jesus, acted no less than would a broken-hearted lover.

Another temple market scourging would happen very near the end of His time on earth. Like a pair of bookends at each end of His public ministry, these cleansings made His message clear. The second one occurred soon after His dramatic and acclaimed entry through the prophetic eastern gate. At that time, He rode in as a humble king on a donkey. This, too, had been prophesied to happen to the promised Messiah. Past kings' coronations began with this traditional donkeyride into Jerusalem through the eastern gate. If the king came gently—crowned during a peaceful time—a donkey was used. If the king came as a conqueror—he rode in upon a horse. Many Passover pilgrims had hailed Jesus that day as their promised Messianic King— who, this time, came to Zion gently, as one Messianic prophesy foretold: "Say to the Daughter of Zion, 'See, your king comes to you, gentle and riding on a donkey, on a colt, the foal of a donkey.'" (Zech. 9:9) The exuberant crowd that praised and ushered Him into Jerusalem were unaware that within days this gentle king, the King of Kings, would be their Passover lamb and wear a crown of thorns.

Jesus was the expected One—deliverer, prophet, priest, and king who was prophesied to be like Moses and, like him, rise up from among His own people. About Him Psalm 24 was written: "Lift up your heads, O you gates! And be lifted up, you everlasting doors! And the King of Glory shall come in. Who is the King of glory? The Lord of Hosts, He is the King of glory." Mostly unrecognized, Jesus was rejected by the religious leaders who were too self-assured to see. Jesus just wasn't what they expected. To them He spoke His last public words, following the second market scourging. The saying puzzled His own disciples as well as His enemies. It was a showdown. His enemies demanded that He tell them where He got the authority to do such things. They wanted Him to show them a miraculous sign to prove His authority came from the Lord God of Israel. Yes, He would oblige them with a sign from God, but they wouldn't understand it. Boldly, He answered them with a challenge which, at the same time, would be the miraculous sign for which they asked. With calm certainty in His voice, Jesus countered the accusations of the merchants, temple guards, Pharisees, and scribes: "Destroy this temple and I will raise it again in three days."

They didn't hear His words to be what they were: a dare and a prophecy. They thought Him to be a fool. All they could see was that He set Himself against them and "their" temple. His words were thought to be a madman's. They didn't know He spoke of His own body as the temple, and that He would raise it in three days just as He had said. Yes, that was the sign that gave Him the authority to do these things.

The new temple would be a spiritual temple, raised up and glorified. Jesus would be the first of many to be so raised and glorified. But not until after the destruction of the earthly, Jerusalem temple in 70 A.D. would people better understand. The Romans would level the beautiful temple and most of Jerusalem with it. Eventually, the biblical teaching of a heavenly Jerusalem and our Lord's spiritual temple here on earth would take on powerful meaning. This became deeply meaningful for believers whose religious life focused so much on the temple ritual and tradition. The spiritual temple, the Church, would be at once mystical, yet also here on earth, with Jesus the head and cornerstone, His apostles the foundation blocks, and all believers the rest of the "building".

Jesus courageously endured misunderstanding in order to accomplish His mission. In fact, these very words were the final blow to these misguided leaders, words that paved His journey to the cross. How could they have known their true Passover Lamb had just presented Himself at the temple—or that they had "sold" Him like the lambs marketed in the courtyard? He was to be slain for their salvation, the ultimate sacrifice for sin. Wasn't that, after all, the age-old reason for these temple rituals? Even His own disciples had not understood what He meant at the time, and they barely began to understand the concept after the temple of His body had been resurrected. Much later, the disciples found in the Scriptures a prophecy regarding this act: "Zeal for Your house consumes Me, and the reproaches of those who reproach You have fallen on Me." (Ps. 69:9).

The first courtyard episode was Jesus' action-filled message that early in His public ministry made Him immediate enemies. The very religious leaders who should have welcomed Him in great joy vehemently turned against him. After His task was accomplished, He slipped away with some of His disciples and left the temple.

Nicodemus, a devout Pharisee, hastily made his way up the many steps leading to the temple. He passed Jesus, not noticing Him. However, many nodded when Nicodemus went by, reverently stepping aside to let him pass. His was an air of prestige and dignity. The religious garb he wore attracted honorable attention and set him apart from the common people. He was respected by his peers, having earned honor and position within the ruling council of the Sanhedrin because of his wise counsel over many years of service in Jerusalem.

The wide, stone staircase which Nicodemus quickly ascended, led up to the main gates of the temple complex. These stairs had been designed to be uneven, unpredictable, so that one entering into the courts of the Lord would have to watch each and every step or risk tripping. Uneven steps were intentional, so that worshipers would focus and prepare themselves for entering into the temple courts near the Lord's presence.

Nicodemus had these stairs memorized because he had spent decades going up and down them. He was in a hurry because of the commotion in the marketplace. A messenger had sent for him when Jesus started overturning the place. By the time Nicodemus reached the area, he saw only the aftermath from what resembled a violent wind storm or act of war. Shouting, angry merchants were chasing around retrieving scattered animals and elusive doves. Some were arguing over whose money was whose that had spilled on the ground. Many were still cursing because of their broken cages and tables.

As Nicodemus walked through the debris, outraged, angry voices accosted him. "We're all just trying to make an honest shekel," a moneychanger yelled. "What are you going to do about it?" another demanded. The angry voices looked to him for justice and retaliation. Within the hour, he met with Caiaphas, the high priest, regarding the incident. At the request of Caiaphas, Nicodemus agreed to keep a watchful eye on Jesus for the remainder of Passover week and report anything he thought to be significant.

Lately, Nicodemus had been hearing things about this man, Jesus from Nazareth. The Pharisees and scribes were all talking about Him and another itinerant preacher, John, who wandered in the wilderness and baptized crowds of people. Jesus and John were separately rumored to be the promised Messiah. John's father, Zechariah, was well remembered by them because he had served many years as a temple priest. There was a rumor going around about John's miraculous birth. No one knew much about Jesus' background, but lately He was causing an even greater stir among the people than had John. Jesus had been seen with the desert preacher and was involved somehow in the repentance and baptizing activities which most Pharisees and scribes scorned.

The next day after the uproar at the temple, a group of people had gathered to hear Jesus teach in a temple side court. A temple guard informed Nicodemus. He went immediately to see for himself this notorious Nazarene. A couple of his closest collegues went with him. They tried to look inconspicuous as they stood a short distance from the crowd gathered around Jesus.

Nicodemus' first sight of Jesus left him unimpressed. In fact, he couldn't distinguish the teacher from His disciples until he asked someone which of them was the Nazarene. Jesus was nondistinctive. His accent was Galilean. His clothes were traditionally middle-class Jewish. His tunic the color of natural white wool. Sandals were laced up over His ankles and disappeared beneath the tunic. Over his tunic was a long seemlessly woven prayer shawl. Fringe dangled at the bottom on its hem, midway between the knees and ankles. Blue woven stripes decorated the shoulder-drop sleeves. Prayer cloaks were traditionally worn by all Jewish men when in Jerusalem for the feasts, or at their synagogues, and while traveling. A braided cord of blue was tied around His waist on the outside of the prayer cloak. Long knots and blue knotted fringe dangled longer than the rest of the fringe at the corners. This was to remind its wearer to pray and keep the Lord's commandments. Made of a fine, soft weave, Nicodemus thought that the prayer shawl was the most noteworthy thing about Jesus' appearance.

Average build, medium height. His beard was long and neat. Medium-brown hair with sun-lightened highlights was parted in the middle and shoulder length, with the exception of one long, streak of hair flowing from the back of His head down the center of His back, in a kind of unbound pigtail. Facial features were characteristically semitic: thin nose, high cheek bones, large luminous eyes, thick arched eyebrows, dark olive skin—Nicodemus judged, was likely from working outdoors.

Certainly, Jesus was not at all the flamboyant, charismatic man Nicodemus had expected. How could such a person as this cause so much contention? As Nicodemus watched Him interacting with those around Him, he noticed that Jesus did more listening and nodding than talking. A would-be rabbi who *listens*? Rabbi: that's what His disciples called Him. But who had been His own rabbinic master from whom He could claim teaching authority? How is it Jesus openly spoke to a woman sitting next to Him in what appeared to be a light conversation?

Questions piled up in Nicodemus' mind.

Jesus had a seriousness about Him yet laughed loudly when a young man whispered in His ear. Jesus was young Himself. He looked to be only about thirty. A strong-looking man, Nicodemus remembered hearing that He was a laborer of some kind. A stone cutter or carpenter—yes, that's what he'd heard. What was a carpenter doing teaching in the temple? Nicodemus' curiosity mounted. He wanted to move in closer but, just as he was about to, Jesus urged everyone to gather closer around Him. So, Nicodemus remained at a dignified distance. As rabbis do when they are about to teach, Jesus sat on a small bench that had been brought to Him. Enthralled to hear His interesting stories and graphic parables, most people were rapt in attention—including Nicodemus. Using His hands while talking, bodily gestures dramatized His points. Eye contact was another method. His eyes were piercing and somehow reached within one's soul. Nicodemus felt this even from a distance.

As Jesus began to teach, Nicodemus did not escape His notice. Jesus glanced over at Nicodemus and his collegues and nodded a greeting. He spoke loudly enough that Nicodemus heard everything. Jesus looked his way several times while He taught, but when their eyes met a couple of times, Nicodemus was surprised by how unnerved it made him feel.

Nicodemus could not dispute any point, though more than a few puzzled him. Jesus certainly knew the Scriptures and had a magnetic way of making them personally alive. But, His tone and pointed language said things with such audacity: not the "on the one hand . . . on the other hand" habit of other rabbis. He talked about Adonai, the Lord, as a son speaks of his father. But then, Nicodemus wasn't sure he heard Him quite right. Did Jesus really call the Lord God of Israel . . . "Abba?"

Jesus conveyed profound things so simply. Where had He learned these teaching methods? Maybe He wasn't so common after all. Nicodemus could hardly picture this gentle, dignified man being the same who had destroyed the temple marketplace in minutes just the day before. There were contradictions in this man that were hard to define. There was something about Jesus that seemed almost noble. He thought about a couple of messianic prophesies and wondered about Jesus' heritage. The Messiah was supposed to come from Bethlehem, from the house of David. But Jesus was from Nazareth. No respectable religious figure would be likely to rise from there.

The group broke up and Nicodemus' friends left, discussing what they'd just heard. Nicodemus looked for an opportunity to speak with Jesus. Unfortunately, Jesus was surrounded by others who were taking His attention. Nicodemus knew that if he walked up to Jesus, he would be given priority; but he didn't want to discuss his questions in front of the common people. Nicodemus was about to walk away when he noticed a woman approach the gathering. She carried a boy on her hip. The boy was too old to be carried; the reason, Nicodemus soon deduced, was because he was a cripple. She walked up to Jesus with the boy, and He immediately stopped conversing to acknowledge her presence. She explained, while straining to hold back tears, that she was told He had the power to heal. "Is this true?" she asked Him. He gently placed a hand on her shoulder and His other on the top of the boy's head. Jesus smiled warmly and nodded affirmatively. He took the boy up in His arms and quietly said something to him that lit up the boy's face in a smile, then gingerly put him down on the boy's own two feet and let go of him. At first the boy clung desperately to Jesus, with arms encircling His knees. But the youngster's own legs held him. Surprised, he looked up at Jesus, quite startled by the discovery. Jesus laughed happily at the boy's reaction. His mother cried out in joy. Jesus pried the boy's hands from His cloak, gently turned him around to face his mother, and gestured with His left hand that she should step back a little, while steadying the boy with His right. "Go on, Son, you can walk to your mother. Try it." The boy toddled nervously to his mother.

The boy was healed. Nicodemus choked back tears. The crowd cheered. Laughing in delight, Jesus hugged a disciple, enjoying the miracle as much as everyone else. Nicodemus rejoiced with them, too (to himself). Nicodemus was certain it had not been staged. The genuine excitement on the faces of the mother and son was proof enough. Nicodemus witnessed what up until now he'd only heard rumored—that the Nazarene performed "signs of magic." Nicodemus noted that he would not describe this sign as magic but as a miracle. But, where did that power come from? Prophets of the past had had powers to heal. Could Jesus be a prophet? It had been more than four hundred years since Israel had heard from a living prophet. Nicodemus read about prophets, but to think there might be a living prophet in the flesh, in his own eyesight? Could he dare believe in something so farfetched?

More than ever, Nicodemus vacillated in his impressions of Jesus, but most of them were leaning toward respect. Still, Nicodemus was troubled about Him. He knew Jesus had not been trained by any of the master rabbis in Jerusalem, nor did He have any other teaching authority confirmed by the

Sanhedrin. It bothered him that Jesus would not go through proper channels. This Jesus had an agenda of some kind. What was it? He could see the potential danger this man posed for Israel if He turned out to be a false prophet. It was God's own command that Israel should rid itself of such liars lest God's people be led astray. In the past, false prophets and self-proclaimed messiahs had brought much bloodshed upon Israel. It could be very dangerous to follow this man. Therefore, Nicodemus decided that he would proceed carefully. If Jesus' teaching was in error in any way and, especially, if His behavior violated the Law, then Nicodemus would know He was a false teacher.

Nicodemus needed to find out what Jesus claimed about Himself, and what His aspirations and goals were. At the same time, some of the things he'd just heard Jesus say stirred his heart. Full of questions, he needed to talk with Jesus alone. The Passover week would soon end and Jesus would probably be leaving Jerusalem. He decided to seek Jesus that night. Should he invite Him to his house? But that would cause talk. Better to see Jesus secretly.

God had ordained that every Jewish holy feast would coincide with a full moon. When Nicodemus left his house, the moon softly lit the night sky and dimly shone on the Jerusalem stone pavement. He walked briskly toward the place he heard Jesus was staying. Eventually, his way led to a poorer section of the city and wound through a maze of narrow alleys and streets. He felt uneasy from the curious looks. Pharisees were rarely seen in this district. The farther he moved into the area, the more anxious he felt—so much so that he almost turned back. Finally, he found the house.

Yes, it was confirmed by those standing around outside that Jesus was staying there for the night. Nicodemus knocked on the door and a round-faced, heavy-set woman opened it. She did not hide her surprise at seeing a Pharisee. He told her that he was looking for Jesus of Nazareth and would like to speak with Him—in private. She nodded, nervously turned and disappeared inside, leaving the door ajar as Nicodemus stood waiting. The woman caused some commotion as she walked through the main room telling others that there was a Pharisee at the door. Suddenly, Nicodemus was alarmed. What if Jesus didn't want to see him? That would be terribly humiliating. It was reasonable that He might not. There had been only suspicion shown Jesus by the Jerusalem elders. Certainly, Jesus would have felt that rejection. His worries escalated and he felt extremely awkward and uneasy as he stood outside the doorway.

Within a few moments he saw Jesus coming toward him. Jesus' manner was welcoming as He approached, making His way through several clusters of people sitting on the floor. "Shalom, Nicodemus." It was a warm greeting from halfway across the room. Nicodemus was relieved that Jesus would see him and felt flattered that Jesus knew who he was, although they'd never met.

Jesus joined Nicodemus outside just after He reached for a lantern and, closing the door behind them, gestured to the outside stairway leading to the roof. He explained that they could have better privacy up there. Nicodemus appreciated His sensitivity. Jesus led Nicodemus up the stairs and onto the roof where there was a partially enclosed upper room built on the flat rooftop. It was a poor man's "upper room". It had a thatched roof and two sides of the room had only half-walls made of woven reeds. It didn't keep all of the weather out, but most of it.

As was the custom for many Jewish homes in Israel, upper rooms were used for religious feast days. The Feast of Tabernacles, especially, fit this particular upper room quite well. That was the occasion for which it was built, but then it seemed right to its owners to leave it up so they could use it as an upper room for other feasts and for occasional Shabbas meals when company visited. It was certainly built more permanently than most "temporary booths" were for that particular feast. Usually, the people built a family-sized temporary booth and lived in it for a week—to remember how God "tabernacled" with His people during their forty-year sojourn in the wilderness.

Now it served as this family's "upper room". Nicodemus thought it was a nice place for a talk and he was quite pleased. Nicodemus took note of Jesus' care to observe the proper rituals before entry—lest they defile its space. Both men removed their sandals. Nicodemus placed each foot in a bowl of water by the threshold. But when he reached for the folded cloth, Jesus knelt and dried both of his feet before doing His own. This was a servant's act, not a rabbi's. Nicodemus was surprised, almost stunned.

In the room, they sat on a mat and faced each other. Nicodemus nervously began explaining why he'd come, saying: "Rabbi, we know You are a teacher who has come from God; for no one could perform the miraculous signs You are doing if God were not with him."

Rabbi. Jesus noted this title with which Nicodemus addressed Him. A cordial and respectful beginning. Jesus knew Nicodemus really was seeking truth. How could He show him that the truth he sought was none other than Himself? Could he recognize the Truth right in front of his eyes?

He didn't let Nicodemus finish explaining the reasons why he'd come. "I tell you the truth," Jesus said, "no one can see the kingdom of God unless he is born again." Nicodemus was stumped. These words puzzled and perturbed him. Nicodemus could see from Jesus' expression that He was sincere. He tried to reason, "How can a man be born when he is old? Surely he cannot enter a second time into his mother's womb to be born!"

Jesus answered, "I tell you the truth, no one can enter the kingdom of God unless he is born of water and the Spirit. Flesh gives birth to flesh, but the Spirit gives birth to spirit. You should not be surprised at My saying, 'You must be born again.' The wind blows wherever it pleases. You hear its sound, but you cannot tell where it comes from or where it is going. So it is with everyone born of the Spirit."

Jesus realized His meaning would remain hidden to Nicodemus until after he experienced faith in Him as his own Savior. But after he did, then Nicodemus would know how the "Spirit blows." Nicodemus' own life would bear witness to that.

A little gust of wind caused the wind-chime to sound from the neighbor's roof. Jesus enjoyed its sound because it added effect to His words even though it completely escaped Nicodemus.

"How can this be?" Nicodemus was impatient. Upset. Jesus studied the bewildered, old face before Him. He thought of the painful separation sin had brought between God and man, and how the power of sin and separation would very soon be ended. He thought about how the religion of the day left much to be desired. It wasn't enough to cause them to know, really know, God relationally. At this moment, the curtained veil-of-separation in the temple was like the "veil" over the eyes and understanding of this son of Israel. Nicodemus was staring right into the holy eyes of his Lord but couldn't "see" Him. All that Nicodemus could ever hope for was right in front of him, loving him. He sought answers to his questions. But, Jesus was, Himself, the only Answer that Nicodemus needed—and was so close.

Momentarily, Jesus looked away from Nicodemus, patience rising. It was hard having His words and teaching rejected or misunderstood by religious leaders. The childlike received and understood Him far more easily than these learned men who were supposed to be spiritual guides, God's representatives, to the people. They knew about God, but didn't know *Him.*

Jesus looked again at Nicodemus, intently regarding him, He delved even further into the heart of the matter and pointedly, longingly, challenged him. "You are Israel's teacher, and yet you do not understand these things? I tell you the truth, we speak of what we know, and we testify to what we have seen, but still you do not accept our testimony. I have spoken to you of earthly things, and you do not believe; how then will you believe if I speak of heavenly things?" Jesus' and John's messages from the Father were rejected by the Jewish authorities. This was a momentous hour and Nicodemus and the others were missing it. How could Jesus talk of these deeper matters of the heart and spirit if the simple message that "the Kingdom has finally come" couldn't begin to penetrate their walls of disbelief?

Jesus' tone, almost as much as the audacious words, left Nicodemus with fewer answers and more questions than before he came to talk. Their conversation ended on fairly friendly terms. Nicodemus believed Jesus was a good man and that He meant well. Why he thought so, he wasn't sure. Maybe it was the way Jesus looked at him.

Jesus watched him disappear into a dark corridor between buildings across the street. He lingered alone for a while on the roof praying for Nicodemus and the matters weighing on His heart.

The following year, Nicodemus volunteered to go into Galilee to witness and report back to the Sanhedrin about the actions of Jesus. Joined by a small delegation, Nicodemus was anxious to see and hear more of Jesus for himself. Multitudes were following Him then, and the Sanhedrin viewed the "Nazarene Matter" a real threat. Nicodemus wasn't quick to judge because he couldn't explain how drawn he'd felt towards Jesus. Maybe Jesus really was a prophet. After all, many prophets had been stranger people than Him, with much wilder methods of communication. He knew that from Israel's history. So, he 'd kept an open mind on the so-called "Nazarene Matter".

The delegation dispersed into a throng of thousands in a hilly area along the lake. There Nicodemus saw and heard some incredible things. He watched dozens of wretched, miserable, sick and diseased people come to Jesus for healing. There were lepers, cripples, the blind, demon-possessed, and people so sick they looked close to death. It was such a pitiful sight to see these suffering people. They came from regions far away, even beyond Israel. This rabbi was healing them. This much of what the Sanhedrin had heard was true! He was a miracle worker of great proportion and, amazingly, He touched the lepers with no reservation or fear for Himself at all. The demon possessed were freed and transformed by His command. Jesus clearly loved each one He saw. Nicodemus saw it in His eyes, in the hugging and touching, the kind words and smiles, in His acceptance and friendliness even toward the most dissipated sinners. He saw that Jesus' every action was love, mercy and kindness. Compassion and joy radiated from Him. Nicodemus spent from morning until evening quietly absorbing the experience of Jesus' ministry to all those who came to that hill of refuge upon which Jesus poured out Himself.

Nicodemus felt strangely blissful—like the God of Israel had drawn very near His people again. It was a life-restoring presence. He felt joy and faith well up inside of him as he sat there in awe of everything going on around him. Most certainly, this Jesus was a prophet.

That Galilean hillside was a beautiful place just to "be". What a tranquil relief from Jerusalem's clamor. Nicodemus was getting a taste of heaven. The panoramic view of the sea, the green, rolling hills, the blossoming trees, relaxed him. The wispy breezes and the distant speckled ports, boats and hazy ridges made him want to be quiet and just look. It was nice to stop all the thinking, thinking, thinking for a few minutes to just enjoy God's beautiful creation.

This was where Jesus loved to teach. It was a practical setting for God's work. Not only beautiful and peaceful, it provided excellent natural sound acoustics. There were some trees and natural stone terraces. The hill was grassy this time of year, and scattered wildflowers grew in abundance.

Nicodemus especially liked the red poppies. There was a cluster of them bouncing joyfully near his spot on the ground. Refreshing breezes reminded Nicodemus of what Jesus had said to him privately about the wind and being born-again.

When Jesus began walking in the midst of them in order to position Himself halfway down the gradual slope, the multitude grew silent. Many of them had been waiting for hours to hear Him speak. They knew this was His custom after some time of healing and ministering to the sick and troubled. The air of expectation was thrilling for all, except a few Sanhedrin spies whom Nicodemus managed to lose in the crowd shortly after their arrival. Most everyone gave full attention to the simply-dressed man standing among them. Jesus' inner virtue almost shone from Him. Extending His hands out to all of them in blessing, He slowly rotated in place, praying heartily for the throng of people there with Him. Jesus knew the exhilaration they felt because so many people had been healed. Then He began to sing a Psalm in a rich, baritone voice. He flung His hands outward, lifted His face to heaven, and began to sing with gusto, giving Himself entirely in worship to His Father. His singing was joined by almost everyone, including Nicodemus. Nicodemus had never experienced this kind of worship in the temple in all his days. This multitude celebrated their God. It was an exhilarating experience Nicodemus would never forget.

Jesus often changed body positions while He taught. He walked a bit, sometimes sat on a boulder, and casually used "natural props" to illustrate meanings. Emotion filled His voice, and His face, often expressing even more than His inspiring speech. Nicodemus was struck by His wisdom. His words were at once gentle yet piercing and were finding their way deep within his own heart. It was as if something old and dead within him were coming alive, a sense of the Lord God of Israel's love—that he had felt when a young boy.

This man speaks from the very heart of God with such compassion and wisdom. He is a master at using parables to convey profound insights and connecting them to people's everyday experience. So much that He says provokes questions. Yet, He also speaks of simple, ordinary things. Who is this man? Nicodemus' comrades had been so sure Jesus was a false prophet. They actually claimed He got His inspiration and healing powers from demons. Would He get demons' power to drive demons away? That just didn't make any sense. No, he believed that the Lord God had to be with Jesus. Only the Spirit of God could make this tired old heart feel new.

That day on a Galilean hillside, Nicodemus discovered what it was that drew him to Jesus despite his inability to fully understand Him. It was how Jesus embodied God's birth-giving, life-restoring, compassionate love. Jesus was a man of great character and passion. Jesus was full of life and love. Nicodemus made the decision to follow his strangely-warmed heart rather than his analytical mind. He still had questions. Even so, he became a follower of Jesus. He had not sorted out what of Jesus' teaching he would believe. Instead, he would trust Jesus and believe in *Him.*

Prayer Journal Exercises:

Here's your invitation to the "upper room" with Jesus. Be expectant. Come and knock on its door. He will open it and meet with you just like He did a long time ago with Nicodemus. Choose all or any of the following reflections. Pay attention to whatever "stirs" your heart to do.

1. Keeping in mind this chapter's gospel account of Nicodemus' experience, reflect on your own personal story (faith journey) of how you have come to know and be nearer Jesus. Make a line graph, or an outline, in your journal to help you.

2. In your journal, sketch or color a picture that depicts your relationship with the Lord at this time in your life. Be open to images or symbols the Holy Spirit might give as you pay attention to your own heart and His.

3. Isn't it amazing: God created you to love you? Just as amazing: no one can love Him the way you can, and no one else can satisfy His desire for you. Using your journal, be open and reflective to the things He brings to mind and think about how, specifically, God has revealed His love to you.

4. In your journal write a letter to Jeus telling Him what it has meant to know Him.

5. Quietly sit in the Lord's presence and ask Him what your relationship means to Him. Write down, in faith, whatever thoughts come to you from Him.

6. Perhaps your faith in God is more doubt than anything else. Write in your journal about how you feel. Do not be afraid to be honest. Jesus knows what it's like for us.

Chapter Two

THE THIRST QUENCHER

They could be heard coming up the rugged road. Three men were talking as they walked. The steady climb led these three from the Jordan River Valley. At the village well, a teenaged boy thought he'd earn a few coins if the travelers were thirsty. He would fill his own bucket for them since his community did not to leave a bucket at the well for just anybody to use. Unwelcome strangers, therefore, couldn't just help themselves.

The boy quickly fastened his bucket to the well rope and lowered it into the deep, narrow well. Momentarily leaving it to fill, he ran a few yards to peer down the winding dirt road to see how far away the men were. Yes, they were getting closer. He hurried back to the well. After hard cranking, the rope wound around its spool until he had the bucket of water in hand. He untied the rope, and returned to wait where the road straightened out some.

The men approached along the edge of rock outcroppings and brush not far from where the boy stood. He still couldn't see them but could hear their voices. Suddenly, they came into full view. They were Jews! Panicked, the boy dumped the water and ran home. As a Samaritan, he knew enough to stay far away from any Jews.

Jesus, John, and Andrew were on their way home from the Jordan's desert valley. They had been near Jericho, one of the world's oldest cities, beside the desolate mountain range south and east of Jerusalem. Samaria was about halfway from there to Nazareth. Since Jesus planned to go home first, they decided to take the shortest route through the mountains instead of along the Jordan River Valley which stretched north and south all the way to the Sea of Galilee. As the backbone does the length of one's back, the Jordan Valley was the "spine" of Israel's geography, from Galilee in the north down to the Dead Sea.

Major crossroads met between Samaria's two largest mountains near the town of Sychar. But most Jewish travelers avoided the entire area because of strong religious antagonisms against the Samaritans. Feelings went beyond ethnic or regional rivalries: most Jews believed Samaritans to be unclean. Long ago Jesus' ancestors lived here, but now it was Samaritan country. Jews usually used other routes to bypass Samaria, but that was not true for Jesus. He saw no reason to go around the region. It was the most direct route.

The road snaked through contrasting landscapes, through many ranges of hills. Some were bare and rocky, others clothed in green vineyards, dotted by olive trees or laced by terraces winding around the hills. Traveling in a northerly direction they came to the town of Sychar, in a lower valley nestled in between Mounts Gerizim and Ebal. Low stony walls bordered fields and walks leading through little farms and neighborhoods. Sychar's ancient well had originally belonged to the Jewish patriarch, Jacob. On the edge of town, surrounded by trees and other shade vegetation, this seemed like a welcome place to stop for respite after their long upward journey.

Normally, Jesus was in strong physical condition from His hard labor as a craftsman, but His forty-day fast in the wilderness had left Him thinner and weaker than normal. Recovery took time, especially since He had joined John for a short time in the wilderness immediately following His desert ordeal. On the barren hills along the winding creek-like river, John preached and baptized. This is where God was doing His work of preparation and where Jesus began His mission.

The Immerser was Jesus' cousin. While with John, Jesus was elated to see how His Father had prepared everything so well. People's hearts were responding to God's messenger. And Jesus saw the larger picture: the Roman Empire's roads, commerce, and common language would bear the word of God— the good news of the Gospel of salvation—which was prophesied to spread from this tiny, strategically located country, to the whole world. God had set Israel apart for His purposes centuries ago. And, Jesus could not forget the Roman crosses, one of which would bear the Word of God. Isaiah 53 and Psalm 22 described the Roman crucifixion of the Lamb of God (God's work of salvation). God foretold these things in Israel's holy writings. Even Jesus' name meant "God's salvation." It was John who recognized Jesus and His mission, calling Him both Lamb of God and Bridegroom. John pointed to Jesus proclaiming that He was the One who would baptize with the Holy Spirit and with fire. There was no doubt John thought of Jesus as more than a man: "The man who comes after me has surpassed me because He was before me." John first proclaimed the mystery that Jesus is the Son of God. He knew who Jesus was the moment he saw Him at the Jordan. When Jesus stepped into the river for baptism, God claimed His son publicly—with a rumbling voice from heaven. Mixed with the wind it sounded suddenly, clearly, upon hearers' ears. Voiced affection—so pleased with His only son. Jesus would be His voice. His love. Then His Father sent the Holy Spirit, like a dove, down upon Him. Like Jesus, sent directly from heaven. Gently it came. Like a dove, this was a sign. This set Him apart as the One who would bring peace. The harmless One who, in order to save, would step into harm's way. He came to redeem His beloved. The Bridegroom knelt in the waters. He sank into its depths humbly, to be buried in the cleansing waters. (It symbolized His death that was to come.) And, similar to this baptism, He would rise from the waters to begin a new creation. The first of many. Because of it, His bride would wear white. Together, they would rise upon the wings of the wind. Together, they would dance on the waves of the sea.

The only one who knew was John. John called himself the "friend of the Bridegroom." As custom had it, the bridegroom's best friend would deliver any communication between the bridegroom and his bride. This kept them from seeing one another until their wedding day—and instilled great anticipation for them. This custom was also practical: the bridegroom spent their engagement time building and preparing their home.

This foreshadows a heavenly, divine engagement. The Holy Spirit is now the "friend of the Bridegroom." "She" has not yet seen Jesus and, therefore, yearns for her Bridegroom's coming. Jesus now, in a spiritual sense, is preparing a "home" for Himself and His bride. When this eternal abode is ready, He will come for her.

During those days by the Jordan, Jesus was introduced to His "bride." His baptism, His trial and personal preparation in the desert, His voice sounding in the arid land—all was so symbolic a beginning.   This was the first coming of the long-awaited Bridegroom.

Jesus insisted He go down into the waters of repentance, "for righteousness sake," He explained to a bewildered, reluctant, John. John obeyed his master and Jesus humbled Himself before all. Jesus was the promised Righteous One (Jehovah Tsidkenu) of Israel.

Jesus was Jehovah-Shalom, the peace-bringer, that Israel awaited. But His peace was much more than anyone could know at the time. All but John. John knew. John and Jesus exulted in the significance of this shared event as they stood face to face, waist-deep, in the waters of the Jordan. Jesus was soaked, His hair dripping, His body shivering—some from cold, some from excitement. Hands joined across from one another, eyes sparkling, smiles broad, no words passed between the two men after the heavenly voice and Spirit-dove had made their statements.

John proclaimed many mysterious things about Jesus to those at the Jordan. Jesus stayed there a few days, met His first disciples, and later went into the desert for a forty-day fast.

Now, heading back to Galilee generated a sense of new beginnings. Jesus was happy to return home for a visit. He hadn't done much traveling, except when He was very young. Just trips for family events and to Jerusalem for the holy feasts. He wasn't used to being away this long. He missed His family, friends, job, and daily routines. Life as He'd always known it was changing forever. His anonymous days as an ordinary Jew were about to end. Most of His close friends were married and raising children. Ironically, it felt as though He was finally getting engaged. It was an accurate feeling. In a sense, His own "bachelor" days were coming to an end. Deep within, Jesus knew this. He thought of the wedding in Cana that was coming up. A cousin was getting married soon. Jesus was glad that the timing of things worked out so that He could attend. Yes, a wedding would be nice.

As the three of them neared Jacob's well, Jesus was telling John and Andrew about the groom's family. Wedding invitations would certainly include Jesus' house guests. Their conversation turned from talking about a family and wedding feast to the present hunger they all felt. They had only a little crusty bread left and that was all.

They were discussing what food they would buy in town when Jesus eyed the well and drifted away in thought. He walked over to it and sat down. With legs stretched out and crossed in front of Him, He wedged His small, traveling bag as a cushion behind His lower back and leaned against the short, stone wall of the well.

Jacob's well was a sentimental place. Jesus recalled the history of this covenant-well. With this well, the Lord God of Israel had made a covenant with Jacob and his descendants. The well represented a sacred pledge of faithfulness between the Lord God of Israel and Jacob (Israel). Jesus reflected on what this well meant to the people who drank from it. From ancient times until the present, this well had sustained lives. It was the only draw-well in the entire region. Therefore, the well had been a sign of God's provision and care for His people.

In a spiritual sense, the well was a lot like Jesus. Jesus would become a covenant "well" between God and His people. How sacred were these moments when Jesus came and sat beside the well to rest.

Eventually, Jesus realized Andrew stood over Him and had been speaking to Him. Jesus' reverie broke and He looked at Andrew with a coy expression, realizing He'd missed something. Andrew asked Jesus, again, if He was ready to go into town. Jesus said He'd rather wait for them at the well. Andrew teased Jesus that He shouldn't trust them. Their money bag was light and not much of a match for their empty stomachs. What if there was nothing left for Him by the time they returned? Jesus smiled and waved goodbye. (If they only knew. The "Bread of Life" was hungry. The "Living Water" was thirsty. Almighty God, in human form, was tired.) Jesus listened to them laugh and joke as Andrew and John disappeared around a bend. He smiled to Himself as He covered His head with His prayer shawl.

This bit of solitude was a great need. He shifted His weight against the well stones, repositioned the bag for better comfort, crossed His arms over His chest, and sighed deeply. It felt good to give Himself to attentive prayer. It was a simple joy to just sit. They hadn't rested much since leaving early that morning. His legs ached and His feet hurt. But, He was more than physically drained because the days preceding this journey had taken their toll on His emotions. He had a lot on His mind. He stilled Himself before His Father and rested.

Jesus had decided to leave for Galilee when news reached Him about how disturbed the Pharisees were about His activities. For months, unending crowds had come to hear John and be baptized. When Jesus returned to His cousin from His forty-day fast, they worked together for a while until Jesus set off to begin His own ministry nearby. Jesus followed John's example and began to preach for the first time. John and Andrew did some of the baptizing while Jesus spoke to the crowds. Word about these meetings spread fast and wide. John had been the real draw. Who wouldn't travel to see a prophet? People were desperate for words from God and were looking for both the Messiah (who would be like Moses), and the Messiah's forerunner, Elijah. Their Scriptures promised that Elijah would come right before the Messiah's appearance. The religious leaders strongly doubted John was a prophet at all. But now they had two imposters! This was getting out of hand. Thousands of people believed both of these desert preachers were from God. How could they stop these growing threats to their authority? There were too many sects and factions already. The common people were so easily deceived.

There was trouble brewing but Jesus wasn't about to let it thwart His growing ministry. It was time to move away from the vicinity. It was too close to Jerusalem, and the Pharisees and their allies had a lot of power. He headed homeward to Galilee where there would be less interference. He would fulfill the prophecy: ". . . in the future He will honor Galilee of the Gentiles, by the way of the sea, along the Jordan. The people walking in darkness have seen a great light; on those living in the land of the shadow of death a light has dawned."

His decision to return to Galilee was confirmed immediately. John had just been arrested by Herod. John's preparatory groundwork was complete. Jesus' time of ministry had come. He also knew a mountain of work lay ahead. And so little time.

His cousin's imprisonment saddened His heart a great deal. But Jesus' trust in His Father stayed His emotions. Jesus knew everything would work out for good. Besides, He acknowledged, the news about John was a familiar pain. Prophets experience this pain. He and John would be no exception. In a way, it was bittersweet. Eventually, the outcomes would make it all worthwhile for both of them. Another pain Jesus felt was in the stomach of His soul. This hunger could only be satisfied by the spiritual harvest which lay ready throughout the land. That harvest would soon satisfy some of this hunger. He was about to taste what no other human being knew anything about. His true food. Bringing people into Himself, by God's grace and through their faith, was His true spiritual food.

Here Jesus sat, at the well, the covenant well God gave Israel long ago. But He had nothing with which to draw water. Jesus is the true living water that quenches our deepest cravings and thirsts. What a wonder. The Creator, who set the oceans in place, who positioned gates and deep holds, deep pathways, and boundaries for the giant waves, the One who sends the rain, and stores water in storage places within the earth, the One who makes the rivers and streams flow, the One who feeds the lakes and ponds with springs, the One who forms the snow, the ice, and the dew, this One who sat beside a well—was thirsty.

A drink of water from this well surely would be good right now. He wondered why a bucket wasn't at the well for thirsty travelers. The only water He and His disciples had left—in a water skin—just walked off to town dangling from John's belt.

A woman approached the well. He didn't notice at first that she carried the needed bucket. It was her fallen countenance, then her large water jar, that captured His attention. Why would she come to the well this late in the day? Then revelation knowledge came to Him from His Father and He knew her pain and needs. He knew her painful past and the heartache she bore. His heart went out to her, full of compassion. Then, He had a wonderful thought. Wasn't it time to make this a covenant well again?

Because the morning trip to the well involved socializing among the women, she always came later. Their stares, whispers and muffled giggling were too painful. She bore the brunt of gossip for the whole town.

She'd had five husbands and was currently living with

someone, an out-of-town merchant she expected would eventually leave her. She'd like to be married to him, if only for security, but the other marriages hadn't given her much security. She'd decided not to care anymore about marriage. Why should she? Hers ended in heartache and divorce anyway. Commitment? She despaired of that. Men just took hers and gave none in return. Romance and love, and growing old with someone was a lost dream. She started young, rushing her dream. All she ever wanted in life was love, acceptance, and security and those were the very things she lacked. The first rejection simply set the stage for many to follow until her reputation preceded her. She certainly couldn't undo the past and the future was out of her control. There was nothing left to do but make the best of things. She stayed to herself and lived one day at a time with no expectations of ever finding the kind of happiness she sorely craved.

She saw Jesus sitting there. She felt uneasy and wondered who He was. As she drew closer, she could see He was a Jew. He wore traditional Jewish clothes. He was removing the covering from His head when she stepped up to the well. He smiled politely at her and then looked away. He seemed quiet and respectable enough and she was relieved He didn't stare. People's stares had become such a painful daily experience. This stranger knew nothing about her. She thought.

As she attached the rope to her bucket, Jesus got up and stood beside her. "Will you give Me a drink?" His tone was not demanding, but the question greatly surprised her. This man dressed like a religious Jew. Why would He break their social and religious rules? He must be dying of thirst. She replied, "You are a Jew and I am a Samaritan woman. How can You ask me for a drink?" Her bitterness against men flavored her words. But she wasn't at all prepared for what He said to her next.

The bucket splashed deep in the well and she began to crank it up. "If you knew the gift of God and who it is that asks you for a drink, you would have asked Him and He would have given you living water." Jesus was about to drown her bitterness and soak her heart in pure love. Jesus said, "gift of God". That's not something one normally says about oneself. Jesus was a humble man. But more, He was a man of love. He knew what she needed.

Speaking with Jesus, she was given the opportunity He offers to everyone He loves and meets, the opportunity to receive true Living Water that only God can give. He's offered Himself to thirsty souls in every land throughout the ages.

Like the metaphor He used with Nicodemus, that of being born again from God's love, this metaphor spoke directly to the moment at the well. Could she recognize Him? Like the wind that brought the recognition of God's life-giving Spirit to Nicodemus, could water bring that recognition to this poor, abused soul? She was a sinner like Nicodemus. She, too, needed the Truth—the true and loving God.

For a Samaritan woman no less than for Jews, this was a real "leap." They were used to analyzing, heeding, rejecting or following a rabbi's teaching. But now, like Nicodemus, she was squinting into the sun. His message was the light, but He was the sun. Clearly, *He* is the center of His message—faith's focus, hope's promise and reward, love's source and sustainer.

As she lifted the filled bucket up from the well, Jesus explained that whoever drinks the well's water would be thirsty again, but whoever drinks the water He gives would never thirst again; for the water He gives would become, in that person, a spring of water welling up to eternal life. She thought He was thirsty, but He knew of her real and deepest thirst. Jesus knew God's Triune Presence was the "covenant well" that would satisfiy all she needed to live—now and eternally.

God speaks of this life-craving thirst and of His being the living water in an Old Testament passage. In Jeremiah 2:13, He said, "My people have committed two sins: They have forsaken Me, the spring of living water, and have dug their own cisterns, broken cisterns that cannot hold water." The people of Jeremiah's day chased after the things of this world. They had forgotten Him. They had other gods and didn't think they needed Him. They had dug broken cisterns they tried to fill with things they thought would make them happy.

Jesus knew this woman had never experienced the living water He offered. She never knew the God of Israel. She, too, had dug her own cisterns. They had broken every time and she was thirsty. Her cisterns had been the six dead-end relationships. She looked for inner needs and desires to be met by mere men.

Only the divine Thirst Quencher could content her inner being. He is the only One who can meet true inner needs, who truly can be committed to someone forever, who selflessly pledges Himself in divine marriage to a soul, who is the only One anyone can forever depend upon, who can satisfy every deepest longing and hope, because this One makes hearts to fit His perfectly.

He stood before the Samaritan woman and offered her—as He does every soul He meets—Life. Living water. Himself. He offers eternal life and with it forgiveness, freedom, His commitment, His love and acceptance. Free.

What a precious encounter this was in the three public years of Jesus' ministry. It was the only time Jesus openly identified Himself as the long-awaited Messiah. The next time He revealed this to anyone was during His trial (though His Father revealed it to Peter). He reveals Himself as He chooses. He delights in revealing Himself. Those who know they need Him will see Him. ("Blessed are the poor in spirit for they shall inherit the kingdom of heaven.") He revealed deep plans and purposes of God, secrets of the Kingdom, to someone of no reputation. But God does surprising, even shocking things, because His ways are so much higher than ours. She wasn't even Jewish (a little religious shock). She wasn't a man (a little culture shock). She was an outcast and a sinner (are we getting the message?). God loves choosing the least likely. She was just the right one to tell. At just the right spot (a covenant well). He told her the desires of God to be worshiped not in Jerusalem, but in Spirit and truth. This would put her deepest ability to love in the right direction. He revealed that concept to no one else. The Church only later came to this same understanding.

Why did He choose her to tell? Again, because of His love. He simply wanted her to know. Wagging tongues and hateful stares would never compare to history's witness of the honor bestowed on her.

The disciples returned and saw Jesus talking with this woman. Jesus saw their curiosity. They said nothing. They were beginning to know Him. He was unconventional in everything He did. Jesus smiled at them, enjoying their silence, seeing their faith and acceptance. He loved to surprise them.

When they urged Him, "Rabbi, eat something," He refused

saying that He had food about which they knew nothing.

The "harvest" in the land had begun—with the Samaritan woman. His Father's will was for Jesus to harvest a crop for eternal life. That was His food. It is likely that He didn't feel like eating because His appetite was temporarily lost in the excitement of it all.

Jesus was delighted with the encounter at the well. This was His Father's way of encouraging, strengthening, and uplifting Him. He was rejuvenated by the faith of this daughter of Samaria. She ran back to town, leaving the water bucket and jar behind. She had living water instead. An instant evangelist, she brought much of the town back to Jesus at the well and they received Him there. He talked and stayed with them for two days. Many believed.

Believing in Jesus one finds the source of life who sustains the living. One of His names is El (God) Shaddai (Pourer-forth). This is He who comes to our well in daily life and offers His living water. Knowing God is all we truly want. That is eternal life. Like the Samaritan woman, we may not know it. Once we know Him, our entire lives will change. We will experience abundant joy, meaning, and fulfillment. It is a wonderful love relationship we can enjoy with Him. We were made to drink of God's very life. Himself. He is the great Thirst Quencher.

Prayer Journal Exercises:

1. Many people are spiritually thirsty. Our parched and weary souls long for true living water. We often neglect the deepest aches within our hearts. We try to fill our spiritual needs with earthly "drink". Like the deer pants for pure, refreshing water, so we long for our God. Often, we overlook growing cracks in our cisterns, or are unaware that putrid waters are seeping into our wells. Can you think of some distractions that keep us from the ultimate "good", which is Jesus Himself?

    * Too much of ourselves given to our houses (earthly real estate) that pretend to be "home"
    * Clothing that will never make us who we really are
    * Classy, fast cars or careers that make us feel that we're really going somewhere
    * "Toys" that preoccupy us and keep us from enjoying what's real
    * Social climbing/status that make us less than we truly could be
    * Addictions of any kind—illusionary liars that keep us blinded to what we truly need and want
    * Low self-esteem because we base our value on what we do, rather than who we really are (precious, gifted, unique, and God's beloved).

2. The Samaritan woman at the well said, "He told me everything I ever did." This is what convinced her He was the Messiah. Why did Jesus bring up the fact that she'd been married five times and now lived with a man? Was He saying, "I will prove you are a sinner. Get right with God."? Rather, wasn't it more like: "I know you are 'thirsty' because you have been looking for love and fulfillment in the wrong places."? That's the heart of the matter. This makes the episode really freeing. Jesus stands at the doors of our hearts and says: "I can deeply satisfy you, now, and forever. Will you drink My living water? Prayerfully imagine you meet Jesus at the well. He asks, "What do you most want? Where have you been looking for love, acceptance, contentment, and security outside of Me?"

Chapter Three

Embrace The Mystery

*T*he Incarnation. God-with-us. Wonder of all wonders is our extravagant God in love. Boundless and beautiful, the Creator bursts in like a wonderful madness in His storms of love upon us. Who can understand the reason why God loves us so? Perhaps the answer lies in who He is.

Mystery was revealed. God became human. He emptied Himself that we might be able to grasp hold of Him. Jesus came that we might know God's wondrous love. That we might know *Him.*

God's desires to love and be loved drove Him to such incomprehensible extremes. These extremes show the distance He's come to pursue His beloved. He wants to be seen and embraced. He knows it's all we truly want, too. For us, that's what the incarnation was—and is—all about.

The great Thirst Quencher thirsts to be thirsted after—to be known and loved. He'd given the written word long before His incarnation. But, it was incomplete. He tried expressing Himself through His relationship with a people set apart as His own. But religious rituals and practices only paved the way for Him (still does). Even what was historically known about Him wasn't enough (still isn't).

Stepping into time, the Eternal One outfitted Himself with arms and legs, put on a face, and visited us in person. He dressed Himself in earthliness. The invisible became solid, thus less real in appearance, for the sake of our eyes and hearts. The All in All became a tiny, tiny seed and planted Himself. The creator of the universe found Himself stretching and kicking against the walls of the womb of a young Jewish virgin. The Light of the World was formed in a secret, dark place which took nine ordinary months. El Shaddai received life-sustaining nourishment through an umbilical cord. And the great I Am suddenly had a birthday.

The way He came to us expressed His extravagance. It was extravagant to bring royalty from afar for a baby shower, to shine a bright new star in the heavens, to give an angelic laser concert for sheep. It was His birth announcement. Though few noticed then, a great portion of the world celebrates this event today. Amidst colored lights, parties, the sending of cards and letters, gift giving, family reunions, and friends expressing joy and love to each other, we celebrate the incarnation of Jesus the Messiah. It marks the coming of God's love to earth—the beginning of His kingdom among us. One dark night, in Bethlehem, as prophetic writings foretold, the Light was born.

It's hard to believe that the King of the Universe began His days on this planet with a bad reputation, even before He was born. He was thought to be illegitimate. But this miracle Child was how God chose to present Himself to us. While whispered gossip flew, the dust continued collecting on the prophetic scroll that foretold the Messiah's birth to a virgin in Bethlehem.

He was the Truth wrapped in a receiving blanket of misconceptions. The way He came to us appeared upside down, but He really came to turn everything right side up!

O, the humility of our God! The King of Kings was born in a cave-like barn. It was in an animal feed box that His face was first seen. His Majesty lying on straw. Nervous parents and bewildered shepherds were the first to greet the King of Kings. Rags wound around Him and flies buzzed about His head. But there, lying on hay, was the face all mankind has yearned to see throughout the ages.

He took us totally by surprise. Divinity in diapers? The designer and engineer of the universe painfully cutting teeth? The shaper of mountains learning to crawl? El Elyon, the Most High God, wobbling to outstretched arms? The statement and expression of the All in All learning to talk? What was His message to us? What does all of this really mean? Why did He surrender everything, both heavenly and earthly, to make it so clear to us? Is it actually because He'd rather die than live without us? If so, doesn't it seem He has more love than wisdom? Maybe that's the main point. His love is the wisdom. He wanted to convince us with it, lavish it on us, and dazzle us with it.

Baffling contradictions surround Jesus from the manger to the cross. Shrouding Himself with simplicity, His glory shone brightly through humility. He came as a humble servant who surrendered everything, both heavenly and earthly, to reach out to us, to save us. His coming was foretold as a promise. But love incarnate extraordinarily became so ordinary that few recognized Him.

Even the obscure and unknown early years of His life speak profound truth. The light that brightened the darkness was a hidden glory. He seemed as ordinary as His neighbors, worked for a living and went to the local synagogue, where His life was so convincingly common that few there believed He was a prophet, let alone the Messiah. His Majesty blended right in. So much like all of us, yet so unlike us. So down-to-earth, yet not of this world. Today, we embrace the contrasts because through them His profound love is revealed.

He exchanged His glory and crown for scorn and thorns. Our joy-giver sighed and cried. The God of love looked hatred in the eye and felt rejection as hate waged war on His love. The most passionate act of love was displayed when our courageous savior defended us with weapons of forgiveness, gentleness, and His own surrendered life. In strength our champion chose weakness, using His almighty power to succumb. His holiness was shamed, our healer was wounded, our comforter was abandoned and betrayed, and the giver of life died for us. Jesus, our refuge became our refuse. He wasted Himself to save our wasted lives. Wisely, He invested. Spending His life to buy ours, He deposited His life in our savings account. The seed of the living God died and was planted in the earth. His tree of death became our tree of life.

He is a God of great paradox. This paradox helps us to really see. His wisdom shines in the obscure. And, His awesome presence hides in the ordinary. We must embrace the contrasts which measure His love because then we can see Him in reality: He is an extravagant, tremendous lover who gives everything He has, and is, for love.

The greatest pilgrim of all traveled from an unimaginable distance in search of His beloved. The shepherd seeks His lost sheep. The parent searches every avenue for a lost child. God-with-us is brokenhearted until He finds each one. Undaunted by the bitter-joy sacrifice of desire, the Lover seeks to win the affections of the beloved until love is returned.

God often hides in darkness until desire for Him is ignited. Then desire itself becomes as a flame in the darkness and illuminates God's presence. His love and glory can be seen and known by His beloved. It's as though He stands in the dark, His radiance blending into invisibility until desire and love enter in. Perhaps that explains some of the contrasts that surround Him.

Jesus spoke with such audacity, who could bear it? The things He said, though true, no one could dare say. "Then Jesus cried out and said, 'He who believes in Me, believes not in Me but in Him who sent Me. And he who sees Me sees Him who sent Me. I have come as a light into the world, that whoever believes in Me should not abide in darkness. . . . He who rejects Me, and does not receive My words, has that which judges him—the word that I have spoken will judge him in the last day." (John 12:44-48)

People thought He was an outrageous blasphemer, crazy, or true. Even those closest to Him were often awestruck by the signs and power He displayed because He was, in many ways, very much like them. He was a simple, humble man who ate and slept with them, laughed with them, and suffered trials and hardship with them. They were also shocked by the strong words that came out of His mouth. Most people had to ask: "Who is He?" Or, "Who does He think He is?" A person's heart swings in the balance.

Even the temple guards, when told to arrest Him, came back empty-handed. They'd just heard Him say, "If anyone thirsts, let him come to Me and drink. He who believes in Me, as the Scripture has said, out of his heart will flow rivers of living water." Their excuse to the Pharisees was, "No man ever spoke like this man!" Either He was a prophet, or someone they couldn't comprehend, or He was an obnoxious troublemaker. He was paradox and contrasts walking around.

When Jesus said, "Unless you eat the flesh of the Son of Man and drink His blood, you have no life in you . . . My flesh is real food, My blood is real drink, " most of His followers left Him. Why did He say that? Wasn't He, after all, seeking their love? That's the answer. He was seeking their love. Those who loved Him stayed. To the twelve He said, "Do you also want to leave?" There is an explanation worked in that sheds a lot of light on this: "For Jesus knew from the beginning who they were who did not believe, and who would betray Him." (John 6)

These contrasts make us have to stop and think, because they strip away one's own heart and mind and reveal the truth that's hidden there. This gentle lamb roars like a lion and confronts and challenges everyone's heart. He is either a rock of stumbling, or a rock of refuge. The cross of His love leaves no other alternatives. The fact that He is gentle doesn't mean He isn't powerful, and though He sometimes seems far away, He isn't. He is closer than our own breath while His glory fills the universe. That, too, is the incarnation which puts all the contrasts into perfect harmony.

Jesus is the Love Song

*What harmony is found
through His humility and sweet gentleness
with the arrogance of His demands and
the audacity of His claims?*

*What harmony is found
in His compassion for sinners
with the claim to be judge over
the living and the dead?*

*What harmony is found
that fuses eternity and time into one?*

*Yahweh, for all His grace and glory
became purely, in harmony, a man.*

Humility—
"Why do you call Me good?"

Gentleness—
"Woman, where are your accusers?"
"I will give you rest."

Claims—
"I am the way."
"I am the bread of life."
"Before Abraham was, I AM."

Demands—
"Whoever desires to follow Me, must take up his cross and follow Me."

Compassion for sinners—
"Today you will be with Me in paradise."

Fusing eternity and time into one—
"You must be born again to enter into the kingdom of heaven."
"And if I go to prepare a place for you, I will come again and receive you to Myself so that where I am, there you may be also."

In one man, one song—
"And His name shall be Y'shua (Jesus), the Salvation of Yahweh (I AM)."
"He will be called: Wonderful, Counselor, Mighty God, Everlasting Father, Prince of Peace."

In perfect harmony.

Jesus.

It seems that everything God does, because of His own desire to love, causes extravagance to such an extreme that simply stating that fact seems a grave understatement. Nor could He simply tell of His love. He had to show it, had to be and embody it. So, God came the distance. He wanted to be loved for Himself, not just for His extravagant gifts, nor even for His glory. The contrasts truly are harmonized through God's love (Col. 3). He did it all for love.

Pondering His dilemma of wanting to be loved for Himself, the romantic story of King Arthur of Camelot comes to mind. King Arthur falls in love with Guenevere, his prearranged bride. They both wanted love, but their prearranged marriage could very well have no affection or passion in it. They happen to meet alone in the woods before her caravan gets to the castle. He was dressed in plain clothes and introduced himself as "Wart." She fell in love with Wart, not the King. King Arthur was elated because he knew the truth: she loved him for himself, first, and only then as the king. Not knowing who he really was, she could act normally with him. Genuine love occurred.

The man, Jesus, came that we might know and love God. Like King Arthur, He took off His king's glory to find true love. Like Arthur, the man in "plain clothes" was the king.

"The King" went to a party and there performed His first miracle, one aptly described as "sheer extravagance." Of course, no one knew He was God! Yet. No sinner was miraculously redeemed. No disease cured. No heart was turned. No one was saved from either hell, sin, or a bad storm. No, wine was running low at a party. Jesus' mother told Him about it and asked Him to help. The request seemed to surprise Him. Was she out of place for asking? He answered her, "Dear woman, why do you involve Me? My time has not yet come."

It seems understood between them that He could do something about it, but He told her that the wine shortage wasn't any of His business. This suggests that He had no preconception about doing this miracle, and it also infers that He wasn't ready to do miracles yet. Then He does it. Perhaps it was a nonverbal look that said "all right," because she immediately told the servants to do whatever He told them. It may be that we're missing part of the story. This certainly wasn't His idea. It was hers. Once the miracles started that would be the end of a quiet, normal life. Once people knew of His power, they'd be after that. Why His actions speak differently than His word on the matter isn't known. But His actions do speak. Loudly. What did it mean that He turned plain, ordinary water into a humungous amount of choice, expensive wine? So they could have fun? To save embarrassment? Yes.

The miracle of wine at a wedding also holds symbolic meaning. Jesus' first recorded miracle displays God's extravagant kindness. After all, wasn't that what His coming was all about? Extravagant kindness? He came and turned water (plain living) into wine (abundant, wonderful, joyous living). God's love is like that wine. What better place to first pour out such extravagant joy but at a wedding? Maybe the wedding in Cana was but a stage set, a play dramatized. Maybe His Father was the One behind it because it was a miracle also for Jesus' benefit. God the Father intends to extravagantly bestow His best wine, the fullness of His love and joy, upon His Son and Bride for a wedding yet to come.

Jesus, the King of Glory, whose footstool is the earth, was born an infant in a humble cave. The Alpha and the Omega— the Beginning and the End—entered time—being born, dying, beginning and ending—the Eternal One. He burst from the ending the Eternal One once again. Eternity will not be captive within the boundaries of time any more than He would!

The Son has come among us, yet is eternally one in the Father. Though our understanding cannot grasp this, our hearts, through faith and love, can. Only by believing in Him can we know Him. Only by loving Him can we know His love.

We must embrace the Mystery.

Prayer Journal Exercises:

Paradox opens our eyes to see God. Allow all of Jesus' humanity to touch yours and let the awesome mystery of who He is bring you wonder and deeper into God's love.

The following "Black and White Portrait of the Savior" is not intended for quick reading but for meditation. It is a portrait of word-sketches of His image seen through the paradox of His character. The portrait uses His names, titles, and deeds to convey the mysterious contrasts that so magnetically attract our hearts to Him.

This exercise can be done a couple of ways: 1) Read through them all and mark the ones you like, then go back and pray with those selected. 2) Slowly read each one paying attention to what stirs your heart. Each idea presented could become a springboard to meditation or dialogue with the Lord. Move on to the next one when it seems right, and so on. 3) Add some of your own to this list.

A Black and White Portrait of the Savior

Jesus, Word of God, showed us God's face.

Jesus, Sovereign Servant, is the Most High.

Jesus, Israel's surrendered Lamb of God, is the roaring and consuming Lion of Judah.

Jesus, the Light of the World, entered darkness for all.

Jesus, our Deliverer, was delivered up for our sakes.

Jesus, the Ancient of Days, became the firstborn.

Jesus, beloved of God the Father, endured His wrath for us.

Jesus, creator and giver of life, gave up His own.

Jesus, love and life, died of a broken heart.

Jesus, fearful judge, is our merciful savior.

*Jesus, Adonai (our Lord and Master,) washes feet and
hearts.*

*Jesus, the omniscient God, was tortured,
blindfolded, hit, and ordered to name who struck Him.*

*Jesus, who bears the government of the world
upon His shoulders,
stumbled and fell beneath the weight of a wooden cross—
from the weight of our sins.*

*Jesus, our healer, became sick, wounded,
dehydrated, feverish, swollen,
disjointed, emotionally stricken, spiritually broken,
and left to die.*

*Jesus, our counselor and advocate, spoke not a word in His
own defense, and was judged in a mock trial.
His sentence became our release and His silence our defense.*

*Jesus, who establishes families and knits bonds of love,
was misunderstood and ridiculed
even by His own relatives and neighbors.*

*Jesus, the "friend who sticks closer than a brother,"
was betrayed and abandoned by most of His family
and closest friends.*

*Jesus, the Root, the Tender Shoot, the Branch, the Vine,
becomes our Wine.*

*Jesus, designer and maker of the seed,
became the Seed that died,
producing the fruit of Life, and others of His kind.*

*Jesus, the commanding general of the universe, armed with
all-powerful weapons of gentleness, love, mercy, and peace
surrendered Himself—which won the war forever.*

*Jesus, who came to set the captives free, was captured, led
bound and humilated as a criminal
through the streets of Jerusalem,
was imprisoned, convicted and executed.*

Jesus, Faithful One, who promises never to leave us nor
forsake us, and that nothing can separate us from His love,
was betrayed with a kiss.

Jesus, giver of the Law and merciful judge,
became the victim of man's poor judgment.

Jesus, who breathes life into each living soul,
hung on a cross gasping for air and suffocated.

Jesus, who makes the clouds His chariot and walks upon the
wings of the wind,
walked miles and miles and had sore feet.

Jesus, carpenter of heaven and earth, hung a Door;
forever making the way open between the two.

Jesus, the great artist, who paints the colors of joy in spring
and glory in autumn,
for a few hours at midday, one unique spring day,
painted Himself passionate red and the earth dreadful black.

Jesus, whose voice sounds with thunder and lightning,
fire and smoke,
was heard to groan with grief and sigh with compassion.

Jesus showed by His life . . .

That love overcomes hate,
That meekness is strength,
That His Life overcomes sin and death,
That the lowly are lifted up,
That the last are first,
That a servant is higher than the one served,
That the poor in spirit are rich in heart,
That good overcomes evil,
That giving is better than getting,
That His truth frees those in bondage from lies,
That light overcomes darkness,
That faith overcomes fear,
That trust banishes stress,
That humility is higher than honor,
That gentleness softens the hard,
That forgiving brings forgiveness,
That dying to self brings true life,
That the righteous are satisfied even when wronged,
That our emptiness brings His fullness,
That sowing in tears brings reaping with joy,
That hope dispels sorrow,
That in silence is His voice heard,
That His wisdom is revealed to the simple,
That obedience is better than sacrifice,
That rest and prayer brings God's work and power,
That living for His pleasure brings us deep joy,
And that surrendering wholeheartedly to Him
is possessing Him.

Chapter Four

DESIRE AND FULFILLMENT

Scripture tells us that God spoke to Moses "as with a friend." In person. Like us, Moses didn't live during the time Jesus walked the earth but he knew God. Moses' first sight of the Ineffable was God's appearance in the holy, unconsumed burning bush. God was in that "fire." Even the very ground upon which Moses stood became holy. The burning bush became the first of many "mountain top" experiences of divine encounters for Moses. Some of them left Moses with a glowing face.

God stepped out of anonymity and Moses became His humble, close, servant-friend. The beginning of an impressive relationship, Moses became God's man doing things God would want to do were He there in person. Through Moses, God delivered His people from slavery and oppression, gave them the Torah and entered into a special covenant relationship with them.

It was God who wanted the relationship and was its initiator. God trusted Moses and chose him to lead. After forty years of desert life, God suddenly manifested Himself and gave Moses a mission. As a shepherd on the rocks and barren hills of Midian, Moses earned his degree and completed his internship. Spiritually, the long arid years prepared Moses perfectly for his mission. Desert wildernesses have tried and prepared many a holy soul.

When God called him, Moses had been content in his present position. But he was just right for the job assignment God had for His long-term comprehensive plan for the world. At this phase in the plan, God needed a negotiator. God not only had long-term plans for a nation and the world, He had plans to befriend Moses.

Moses lacked confidence in his ability to lead. Yet thousands of enslaved people were freed and led by him. With God at his side in negotiations with Pharaoh, they performed spectacular signs and wonders that certainly must have surprised Moses himself. During those summit meetings with enemy ambassadors, Moses' power leverage was ten plagues sent from God. Of such diverse, vivid and annoying character, surely they baffled all—especially the devil, who tried his best to outdo these signs from God with magic. What an exciting "meet" that must have been for Moses. Another wonder happened when Moses raised his rod and the sea opened wide before the fleeing people so they could pass across on dry ground. (Imagine how Moses must have felt when that happened.) Then the sea crashed to drown their pursuing enemies. How spectacular was God's power through Moses!

To God's beloved people He was present through Moses and, later, in the Ark of the Covenant and the tabernacle. To Moses, God revealed His name, YHWH: "I am that I am; I will be that I will be." So sacred was God's name to the people of Israel that they never pronounced it. Instead they called Him, "ha-Shem," (the Name). That is why no one really knows how to pronounce YHWH. YHWH's name was similar in meaning to Alpha-Omega. The Eternal—right now. And, Moses got to know God on a "first name" basis.

When God said to Moses, "I AM" He certainly meant it. To prove it, God delivered the the Israelites from bondage. Then "I AM" stayed with them, and manifested His presence to them. The Eternal One traveled with them as their guide, protector, and companion. God's presence was in a pillar of fire at night, and cloud by day. These physical manifestations assured them that He cared and was with them. His watchful, warm, glowing-red tower of fire was an awesome nightlight. In the bright daylight hours, His pillar of cloud stayed with them. The cloud also led them when they traveled. One season God sent plagues and lifted a whole sea of water; the next, He quietly gave His Presence in signs of comfort and protection like a mother tending her little ones.

God drew near. The Word of God, YHWH, spoke up. The all-powerful yet gentle, awesomely fearful, yet intimately caring One, came and stayed with His people in the wilderness on the way to the Promised Land. He just wasn't touchable then. (Like how it is with us today.)

Moses was greatly favored by God. To Moses, God became

close and personal. Moses heard God's voice clearly. He met with God in the Tent of Meeting—in the Tabernacle—on a regular basis. God said to Moses, "I am going to come to you in a dense cloud, so that the people will hear Me speaking with you and will always put their trust in you." (Exodus 19:9)

But, after all the powerful things they did together, after all the Tent-of-Meeting talks, it wasn't enough for Moses. Moses wanted more—not from God, but of God. Moses asked to see God's glory. Moses wasn't asking to see more of what God could do. Moses wasn't interested in experiencing more blessings from the "hand of God." At this point in Moses' life, he began to desire God alone. Moses wanted to see God's face.

Surely, Moses' request delighted YHWH. Paraphrased, God responded, "Yes, to a degree." God said to Moses, "I Myself will make all My goodness pass before you, and will proclaim the name of the Lord before you; and I will be gracious to whom I will be gracious, and will show compassion on whom I will show compassion." (Exodus 33:19) But God said to see His face meant certain death. He said, "You cannot see My face, for no man can see Me and live." But God wanted to do what He could, so He said, "Behold, there is a place by Me, and you shall stand there on the rock; and it will come about, while My glory is passing by, that I will put you in the cleft of the rock and cover you with My hand until I have passed by. Then I will take My hand away and you shall see My back, but My face shall not be seen." (Exodus 33:21-23) God granted a great favor to His friend. He gave Moses his heart's desire.

Meditating on this statement can be enlightening. Since it is Scripture, God says it to us today. Breaking it down phrase by phrase can reveal parallels with how we, too, can see God's face—God's glory.

The Mystery Revealed

♦ *You cannot see My face for no man can see Me and live . . .*
Simply, we cannot behold God's unveiled glory.

♦ *But there is a "place" by Me*
This may be a "dimensional, or spiritual place" outside of time-place, in the eternal realm. It is a spiritual reality-place through redemption. For us, this place by Me is "at the foot of Jesus' cross." Could it also be a "place" of prayer?

♦ *. . . and you shall stand on the rock*
Faith and trust in Jesus and His work of salvation. Jesus is the "Rock."

♦ *It will happen that I will put you in the cleft of the rock ...*
I will cause you to abide and be hidden protectively in Jesus.

♦ *. . . and cover you*
The covering that shields us from God's holiness because of our own sinfulness and unworthiness.

♦ *. . . with My hand*
With God's own actions; both blinding our eyes to not see Him and the dying for our sins.

♦ *. . . until I have passed by*
We recognized God's passing by us, Jesus' glory was seen as He was leaving . . . He "covered" our eyes until He had died and risen for us.

♦ *... then I shall take away My hand and you shall see My back*
Then I shall remove the blinders and you shall see Me as I am leaving. Most of His disciples recognized Him after His death and resurrection just as He was leaving. Maybe there are those special times in our own lives when we recognize Him after He's come and He's gone.

♦ *... but My face you shall not see.*
We still cannot see His glory fully. We will someday.

Going back to the first statement, which the second part seems to clarify, God said: "I Myself will make all My goodness pass before you, and will proclaim the name of the Lord before you; and I will be gracious to whom I will be gracious, and will show compassion on whom I will show compassion." Isn't this a perfect description of Jesus' coming? It describes His coming to each of us. Jesus brings grace and mercy to those who deserve no mercy. Those He saves will know and love God forever. They will see God's glory.

Moses literally stood in a real cleft of rock on a mountainside. God may have had global things in mind when He answered his request, but He also had Moses in mind. What a prayer experience! Hundreds of years later, when the Lord put aside His glory and emptied Himself and was seen as a man, Moses' ancient prayer was answered again. It was such a sweet gesture. A Friend was in need of a friend who would understand. Moses joined Elijah and appeared to Jesus during a "mountain-top experience" we call The Transfiguration. Jesus was transfigured while talking with His faithful friends. Moses encouraged Him and they discussed what was about to happen to Jesus in Jerusalem. This wasn't news to Jesus. It was sharing a burden. This time Jesus ended up with the glowing face.

Carlo Caretto says in *The God Who Comes:*

> "God presents Himself to us little by little. The whole story of salvation is the story of the God who comes. It is always He who comes, even if He has not yet come in His fullness. But there is indeed one unique moment in His coming; the others were only preparations and announcement. The hour of His coming is the Incarnation. The Incarnation brings the world His presence. It is a presence so complete that it overshadows every presence before it. God is made human in Christ. God makes Himself present to us with such a special presence, such an obvious presence, as to overthrow all the

complicated calculations made about Him in the past. The invisible, intangible God has made Himself visible and tangible in Christ. If Jesus is truly God, everything is clear; if I cannot believe this, everything darkens again."

(*The God Who Comes* by Carlo Carretto; Orbis Books, c1974. Used with Permission.)

Jesus Himself is the light we grope for, and when He comes our lives become bright, our journeys clear. That's why He came, comes and will come. When God has compassion on each of us, and opens our eyes, we see Jesus. He looks at us, gives us the "eye," and we respond. We will ignore Him, snub Him or love Him.

When it comes to matters of love, love is universal. Especially with God. In *Three Philosophies of Life,* Peter Kreeft emphasizes how life is love.

"We all know this: love must be freely given and freely accepted. 'It takes two to tango', and neither one can be pushed, pulled, dragged, or carried. There are really only three methods of influencing other people, three techniques of 'behavior modification': pushing, carrying, or drawing. You can use force or fear to push people where you want them to go, against their will. Or you can carry them. Then they are passive and you do the job for them, like a parent for an infant. Finally, you can draw them, attract them, motivate them to move toward you by the magnetism of desire. That is what the bride asks the groom to do: 'Draw me after You, let us make haste' (Song 1:4). She will not be His slave and be pushed, or his child and be carried, but His bride and be drawn. He has the initiative, but she responds with equal freedom and equal value. To be drawn is as free a choice as to draw. To come is as free as to say, 'Come'."

. . . It is the hardest thing in the world to be patient about, for it is the thing we need the most and desire the most. But it is also the most necessary thing in the world to be patient about, for if it is not free, it is not love."

. . . People talk a lot about freedom today, much more so than in ancient times. Perhaps that is because they do not know love. For lovers do not talk about freedom: they are free already. They do not desire to be free; they desire to be bound forever to their beloved. To be free from love, free from God, is precisely Hell."

(*Three Philosophies of Life* by Peter Kreeft; Ignatius Press; c1989. Used with permission.)

God can draw, motivate, attract, and kindle desire in us as a means to awaken us to love Him. That also is what Jesus came to do. And why He still comes. But as in true love, we must desire Him. Peter Krefft also says:

'The paradox of love is that it is bittersweet. Its very sweetness is bitter, and its very bitterness is sweet. Both qualities are present in desire. Love's desire, like all desire, is bitter and painful because it lacks what it wants. If it did not lack what it wanted, it would not be desiring it but would be enjoying it. But the very desire is also sweet, a joy, a fulfillment. Merely to long for God is better than to possess the whole world. This absence is better than any other presence; this desire is better than every other fulfillment." (*Three Philosophies of Life*)

Many saints, writers, and Christians of prayer have discovered God in their desire for Him. C. S. Lewis says, "The form of the desired is in the desire." Desire for God comes from God because our Christian spiritual life—our relationship with Him—springs from divine revelation. God's love always initiates ours. God woos us. Deep calls to deep. Deep desire for God, therefore, is a revelation of God. Longing for God Himself is filled with the awareness of God because it is borne from the very revelation of God and His love. Close, personal, affectionate love with the Lord Jesus is the reward for those who receive His. He is the original initiator, but then, in response, we must return love for love.

Jesus is the Desire of all Nations unknowingly groaning for Him. We, too, groan in our inward parts; we long (often unknowingly) because He pursues and woos us. Created for that love we cannot be satisfied until we know His infinite, life-giving, but also affectionate love.

Some favored souls have tasted this heaven and have lived to tell about it. What follows is an imaginative story from one of them, one who knew God's favor and love. It wasn't so much because God favored him over others; it was more a matter that this one wanted and received God's love. How much God yearns for those who will receive it.

When Jesus said "Follow Me," He was serious. You see, all of Israel was waiting for Him. We didn't know it was this Jesus we were waiting for until later. I remember the day I met Him. I followed Him as He walked away from the Jordan. When I caught up to Him, He turned and asked me what I wanted. I didn't tell Him then that He was everything good I ever wanted. Well, I didn't really even know it yet myself. I answered by stammering a question about where He was staying. It was my way of following Him without being asked to. I really wanted to be with Him. Andrew was with me and we knew we'd found a great new friend. Jesus drew me to Himself like a mother hen does her chicks. I belonged to Him somehow. And always will. He knew what we all really wanted: to follow Him.

One thing about following Jesus was that we never stayed in the same place for very long. He surely was that "hound from heaven," all right. Even when thousands were with us, He'd leave them all in search of others in remote places. Once I suggested that we stay and make a permanent camp-facility where people could come to us and that we could call home for awhile. He'd have none of that. I couldn't understand why not; multitudes were with us. It made sense to provide them with a community environment of some kind. No, we who followed Him during that time traveled—a lot!

Come to think of it, when following Jesus one never stays in the same place for very long, does one? Spiritually, I mean.

Fame became an exciting thing. People were so drawn to Him. We just couldn't help ourselves. The miracles were phenomenal. Every town, village, and roadway buzzed with stories. His words were quoted everywhere by almost anyone. But who could believe them? It was something one just had to hear firsthand. And, of course, everyone in Israel had his own—strongly held—opinion. We Jews are known for that.

And, let me tell you, Jesus had no qualms about stating His opinions. Some of the things He said were hard and tested a person's motives and heart to the quick. He had a way of reading people that was uncanny. He knew things about them that could be seen in the way He looked at them, or how He touched them, or by what He'd do for them. He was untiring in charity and patience. But sometimes He'd be so sharp with someone it would startle me. He knew each person's agenda, and would, with a single comment, turn one's whole hypocritical, self-righteous world upside down. I'd watch Him turn into instant stone with certain people. Other times, a moment's glance could cause a melting of one's whole being like butter over a fire. Looks of compassion were the most common of all. Sometimes I'd weep just watching Him with people. His love was so powerful.

I saw plenty of His enemies stomp away from Him in rage. Pharisees were the most common. One thing they really loathed was how sinners came to Him and that He didn't shun them. I think at first the elders thought He was a man of compromise and a sinner Himself; but then when so many sinners started appearing in the synagogues and temple to pray and worship, well, I think it made the religious leaders jealous. The Pharisees wondered how He "reached" them. They never could figure that out. Changed lives were left everywhere He went. How did He do it?

I knew how. He did the opposite of what they did. Instead of snubbing sinners and pointing a finger, He accepted and got to know them. They liked Him and wanted to be around Him, and

His goodness just sort of rubbed off. When they asked for advice or instruction, not before, He'd give it. And, they asked. His answers always spoke personally and directly to each one.

It wasn't like that for those of us that were already His followers. He treated us, His disciples, a lot differently than He did the "sinners." With us, He continuously taught and demanded faith and trust. I always felt like I was slow to understand much of what He was trying to convey. His parables and stories were filled with so much meaning that often I was left mind-boggled. Trying to determine when He was talking literally and when symbolically became quite a challenge. He sometimes seemed impatient because of our slowness to understand or because of our lack of faith. There was never a dull moment with Him. Trying to figure Him out was an ongoing adventure.

Once He called me "son of thunder" after I had made a wild comment suggesting He should strike a Samaritan town with fire from heaven because they had been so rude to Him. He laughed at me and called me that name. He said I didn't know to what Spirit I belonged. Well, I have a better idea now. You see, His Spirit is nothing but love. The closer our friendship became, the more I loved Him. Eventually, I could see that this was no ordinary rabbi-disciple relationship. I felt so closely bonded to Him right before He left us that it is evident to me now that His time had come to return to heaven. I was so drawn to Him. Didn't God call Israel His bride? Didn't our Scriptures say that God was married to us all? I loved Jesus with all my heart. He was everything to me: brother, friend, Rabbi, Lord. My all. I truly would do anything for Him.

The last night we were all together, I sat with my head nestled upon His chest. There I was the most content I have ever been. I heard His heart beating. When He talked out loud, His low voice soothed me into a deep, restful state. I was only aware of being there against Him. My love was pouring out to Him. Did He know? As soon as my mind asked the question, He whispered my name, "John." My name, sounding from His lips, was all love. Oh, my name to be His word said so gently and sweetly. I wanted to stay there forever.

Incredulous! One of us upon His chest and another one running out the door ready to betray. I will never understand Judas. There are many Judases, though. In a way, even I have been like Judas. I've betrayed Him in selfish ways. We are all so unworthy of His love.

I hardly knew who He was then. He walked so often beside me. Looking back, I love to remember Him but I really feel closer to Him today than I did then. We often talk the same way we used to when I'm praying (within me, that is). I can still feel His eyes loving me. I can still see Him doing things for me. Even more so now. Sometimes, I'll be in the middle of doing something, my mind full of the present task, and suddenly, out of nowhere comes this sweet sense of His presence and love—as if, suddenly, He walked into the room. The same way it was back then.

He was right about knowing Him and worshiping Him in Spirit and truth, and that He would be with us always. I remember the day He said that. I was so happy after the hellish thing we'd all been through. He was radiant. He was alive and with us again. My mind and heart couldn't take it all in. Couldn't take Him in! His presence was so overwhelming to me, it seemed somehow a relief to think He'd soon be in heaven. I fully expected we'd all be going there very shortly. I wanted that so much. I don't fear death, I would welcome going to be with Him any time. Yet, here I am in my old age, still waiting. Ah, but even my waiting is full of His presence.

That day before He went up into heaven, He made us feel so loved, so hopeful, so challenged. Our lives would go on, not without Him, but with Him. He assured us of His closeness, no matter what. Well, we believed Him. We believe everything now. Not a word of His would be doubted ever again. I love Him! Sometimes so much it hurts. The thing that I've noticed, that has never changed, is that the more I know Him and experience His love, the more I want.

It's so ironic. Often, I had noticed such a pained look on His face when He addressed people. I never understood it until I felt it myself; only now, I feel it for Him. It's a loving desire that is so strong that it hurts. His love is passionate. A consuming fire. Wonderful. It gives all.

My God! My God! You are all love! Yes, Heaven has come to earth so that we could be in heaven. You know, I think I'll write these things down. I have to find some ink. The Word of God has come and I have seen and touched Him. And still do. Oh, we all can. Come, Lord Jesus. Come, through my words. Come, through Your Word. Yes, come, Lord Jesus! "The Spirit and the Bride say, 'Come!'"

***

Most Christians know about Mary of Bethany's devotion to Jesus. John, in his Gospel, dramatically described her as "the one who anointed Jesus," as if this would quicken the reader's memory to know to whom he referred, even though he hadn't yet told that story and was getting ahead of himself. She was known for her displays of love to Jesus.

This next imaginative story is based upon John's account and is of such sweet inspiration that John would like all of us to simply be like Mary. John knew that this was one of Jesus' most important lessons, even though Jesus didn't teach it Himself. Drawn from an actual experience that happened to Him, Jesus communicated the great significance of this lesson.

Multitudes flocked to Jesus and followed Him. He became a shepherd of thousands. They came to see His miracles and listen to His words. But Jesus didn't let His heart trust their devotion. So much of their interest was not spiritual or even heartfelt. Most were simply self-centered. They wanted Him for what He could do for them. Some wanted to make Him a king for filling their empty stomachs. But He had more than that to give. Jesus wanted to fill their hearts and spirits with Himself and His love. He would be king. But not the king they wanted. They wanted freedom from their enemies, the Romans. But He had come to free them from their real enemies—sin and death. He went beyond—and outside—anyone's expectations. No one could have dreamed that much.

One day they would know. In the meantime, He would be misunderstood.

The religious leaders, who should have recognized and welcomed their Messiah with open hearts, were skeptical and jealous of Him. They pursued avenues of trickery, and looked for ways to trap and defame Him.

No wonder Jesus looked forward to going to Martha's house. He loved Martha, Mary, and Lazarus. They were such close friends. Often, when He went to Jerusalem they opened their home to Him and His companions. They lived on the other side of the Mount of Olives, in a town called Bethany, about two miles from Jerusalem.

Jesus knew His mission was soon to be completed. He taught and healed multitudes, traveling from region to region. He also prepared Himself and His disciples for what lay ahead. It was an exciting, yet trying time, for His group. Not only did Jesus perform miracles and preach but so did His disciples. Jesus instructed them how to teach and what to do by His example. A never-ending river of mankind streamed to them wherever they went. Sometimes His disciples were sent out separately to cover more ground. But always, it seemed, Jesus was surrounded by the needy. Many people hoped He was the Messiah. But no one, except Jesus, knew how the Messiah would set up His kingdom. No one knew how God would save them.

Jesus was glad to finally be in Bethany. He enjoyed being with His friends there. They were most hospitable toward Him. He found in their home much welcome, love, fellowship, and comfort. It was a safe place where He could open His heart and not have to be so guarded.   Because of the many demands made on His itinerant life, He'd had to give up many comforts, even necessities, for the better part of His public ministry. He had found Martha's good meals, a bed to sleep in, and a refreshing bath, most pleasing gifts. But more important, He found real friendship.

They would all gather in one room, and He would share news of the work of the Kingdom. So much was happening. He shared His Father's heart and purposes with them. He laughed with them. Openly, His dreams and disappointments would teach them, as He shared His work and Himself.   He would report events with such emotion, including every detail, telling the full version of each story. Tears would roll down their faces and His—sometimes for joy, sometimes for sorrow. When they were together, they could really be themselves. That's the way it is with people. When important things happen to us, we want to share them with our best friends.

Poor Martha. She was very busy in the kitchen. Mary was in the other room with everyone else, and sat at the feet of Jesus, giving Him her undivided attention. She listened and stayed as close to Him as possible. Absorbing, learning, thinking, watching His every move. She noted every detail in the changes of His voice to catch the ideas of this intense man whom she'd come to know and deeply care for.

From the kitchen, Martha could hear their voices but couldn't catch the words. She had spent too long plucking chicken feathers, and the vegetables weren't washed or peeled yet. The bread was burning outside in the clay oven, she was sure. She remembered that James didn't like cabbage—it bothered his stomach—and she needed to find another green vegetable and wondered if the green beans would be too stringy and tough due to over-ripening. Amidst all the growing tension, she wondered what they were talking about in the other room. After awhile, she became upset over how she was left to do all the work by herself while her sister sat in the other room doing nothing. Suddenly, there was an eruption from the kitchen. Martha burst into the room and interrupted Jesus in the middle of His story. "Lord," she blurted, "don't You care that my sister has left me to do the work all by myself? Tell her to help me!" Her accusation made Jesus look guilty for letting Mary sit there. Martha was angry at Mary and Jesus. In her opinion, it just was not fair.

Jesus was looking down at nothing in particular when He replied to Martha with gentle but loving firmness. "Martha. Martha." Then His gaze went to her eyes as He continued, "You are worried and upset about many things. But only one thing is needed. Mary has chosen what is better, and it will not be taken away from her."

It's hard to get beyond those first two words. "Martha. Martha." There it is: His heart. In those two words. They were spoken slowly, full of emotion. Her name was spoken with profound love and controlled patience, mixed with His own expectations and hope. He so wants our friendship—our hearts.

Her complaint seemed justified. Siding with Martha is what we all tend to do. But here is that unexpected, extravagant love and way of His that brings surprise. Our upside-down sense of priorities when it comes to pleasing God. Martha loved the Lord, too. It was obvious. How hard she worked for Him! She was serving Him—cooking the meal and trying her best to make everything perfect. Just for Him.

He knew that. Jesus loved Martha just as much as He did Mary. He wasn't treating her unkindly. Nor was He unappreciative of what she was doing for Him. But, He was honest with her and taught her (and us) a profound truth.

He prefers our attention, devotion, listening, and sitting in His presence to our being distracted away from Him by busywork. Sitting at His feet, Mary chose to simply be with Jesus.

That's what was on His heart that day in His friends' home in Bethany. He wanted fellowship—a meal of love. Too often we deny the Lord what He hungers for: our attention and devotion. Martha was missing out on the best thing. It really was a kindness He showed her. He lovingly turned her toward Himself and away from all the work and cares.

Time spent at Jesus' feet (listening prayer) will inspire one to serve Him entirely. To be like "Mary" first and "Martha" second will produce holy motives and love in action. Devotion for God alone will create holy servants who will be more in tune with God's heart and His will.

Mary desired to spend that time with the Lord, who had so captured her heart. Her desire brought her into His presence. Without it she might have been out behind the house chasing a chicken for supper. What a missed opportunity it would have been if she didn't choose to sit at the feet of the Creator of the Universe.

Really, how often does God come in and sit down with you in your living room?

This glorious face of Jesus, YHWH the Savior, was the glory Moses had been shielded from seeing while hidden in the cleft of the rock. It was the veiled glory which John so dearly loved. Even John knew that bitter-sweet pain of desire and fulfillment.

We all must, if we are to follow Jesus and love Him. God's great desire is that one day we shall see Him and know Him just as He is, in all His full radiance and goodness. Until then, this friendship with God is "a place by Me" and is eternal life—knowing God and Jesus whom He has sent. What about sitting at His feet to listen and gaze? What about sitting and resting one's inner being upon Him—heart to heart?

The following story is taken from what could be called a meditative vision—an intimate experience with the resurrected Lord.

*J*esus of the Gospels had come long enough to win my heart through the reports of His visit and then disappeared, leaving me to wait until I die to be able to see Him. At least, that's how I felt one morning while away on a personal retreat. My longing to see His face was painful. Perhaps the purest form of prayer is desire for God.

Jesus surprised me.

Did it really happen? It did for me. The Holy Spirit revealed to my imagination a kind of sanctified, meditative experience. Jesus transformed my quiet room to one in another time and place. This time, I was the invisible one.

Jesus was sitting on the floor, thoughtful, elbows resting on bent knees, leaning against a light gold limestone wall. He was with His friends again. They'd just finished eating. Those who had been sitting beside Him had left His side for awhile. They were used to Jesus being with them again after His resurrection, not yet aware that, soon, He would ascend into heaven.

It was quiet with bits of conversation floating throughout the house. Mary, Jesus' mother, came up to Him. As she neared His side, He smiled warmly at her and she sat down next to Him. Such a strange thing to know—and not know—your very own son. Questions and insights were whirling around within her, crying out to be understood and realized.

Her voice quivered slightly when she addressed Him, "Son, I . . ." She saw in her Son's eyes love and understanding and a deeper, puzzling thing she'd often seen there many other times—

an intensity too deep to define. She gathered her courage. "Son, . . . are You . . . God?"

Before venturing over to His side, she had reminded herself of the angel's remarkable words before her virgin pregnancy. His birth had brought brilliant angels and gawking shepherds. Mysterious prophesies by elderly strangers—one was an old, holy woman in the temple at His "Presentation." The foreign, noble seers who brought symbolic gifts and worshiped Him. His innocent and blessed childhood. His responsible helpfulness to her always and her need for Him at home. His "Call," His miracles and rise to fame. His strange teachings in public that finally caused their family to think He'd gone insane. His enemies in high places. His inhumane murder. And, His resurrection. She knew He was the promised Messiah, the King of Israel, the one God would use to deliver them. She knew Jesus was God's own son. But, what did that really mean? "Hear, O, Israel, the Lord, our God, the Lord is one."

I was deeply touched. She grappled with the same things I grapple with—the inability to comprehend His present reality, who He is . . . now. The incarnation of God. Did she understand? Do I?

"Son, are You . . . the Lord God of Israel?" She hoped she wasn't wrong for thinking it. Yet, this is what she had to ask.

A holy moment. Softly, Jesus answered, "I am."

Waiting only a moment, He asked, "Mother, do you remember the little wooden bird I made for you?" This sudden shift surprised her. Warmly, she remembered, and a smile quickly appeared on her face. Yes, she remembered the little wooden bird Jesus gave her years ago when He still lived at home. Only a few years ago, because of her delight over a particular songbird, He had surprised her with a hand-carved replica of it. It was a piece of art, not an idol. It was rare for law-abiding Jewish families to have wooden images in their homes; but Jesus said He wanted her to have it to remind her of God's love, which had sung so sweetly through the little songbird they both knew and heard during those peaceful days.

Smiling, she remembered the treasured keepsake. It was still at home sitting on the window ledge.

Just then, from somewhere or nowhere, Jesus reached behind His back and handed her a live bird—like the kind she loved and He'd carved—a small, round little songbird with a yellow belly. "Here. Go ahead, take him. He's tame." Jesus gently placed it in her cupped hands.

As she took the feathered creature from Him, the realization struck her. "Oh, Jesus! You made this one, too, didn't you?" Warmly, He smiled and nodded a Yes. He watched her hold the little bird and pet him with her finger.

"Mother, what will you do with him?"

She looked at Jesus. "Well, I could put him in a cage." Looking back at the bird, she reasoned, "Oh, but the cage's door would need to be left open . . . But then, what good would a cage do? Oh . . ." Jesus interjected, "Mother," He touched her chin with His hand. She looked into His eyes. "That's what you have to do with Me."

My vision ended. I was struck with a truth: it's impossible to hold on to His Spirit. Jesus comes and goes freely, graciously, like the little songbird. He is God and came in the incarnation to Mary first. Now Jesus—His Spirit—comes to us. Like her, I must hold this Mystery loosely. I know the longing in my heart will be met with His sweet melodies singing about His love for me. I already have heard His singing. Some day I will see Jesus in full glory. Until then, His incarnational and transcendent presence is *His present reality* with me. And, like a songbird, Jesus can enter the open cage of a heart as easily as in a vision.

We were made to enjoy God. We can learn the same lesson from Moses, John, and Mary of Bethany. Desire to see and know God springs from a holy well. We were made to love God with our entire being. This is a holy love, a divine relationship! We are Christ's spiritual bride.

Prayer Journal Exercises:

1. Three types of prayer (dialogue, meditation, and contemplation) are very simply described in the paragraph below:

    Once there was a man who was in love with a beautiful woman. Since they were physically apart at the time, they were writing letters and talking on the phone. (Dialogue Prayer.) Often he would reread her letters, stopping to think about His beloved. He would remember events, reflect on the things she'd said or done. This would rekindle his love. (Meditative Prayer.) Then suddenly, while he was reading and thinking about her, she walked into the room. They saw one another. (Contemplative Prayer.)

    God reveals Himself today through dreams, visions, stories, experience, beauty, words, thoughts, ordinary life events, and on and on. God continually reveals Himself to us as we journey with Him in faith. Getting to know Him fully might take an eternity. For *this* moment of your journey, however, can you imagine God saying the following? "'And you will seek Me and find Me, when you search for Me with all your heart. I will be found by you,' says the Lord." (Jer. 29:13)

    What shape or form is that search now taking?

2. Because Jesus longs for us to know Him, He uses many creative ways for that to happen. He longs for us to know His love! The following step-by-step method can become an opportunity to experience all three forms of traditional prayer experience described in the first exercise.

    Place yourself in a Gospel story with Jesus. Become someone in the story. Or, simply be yourself with Him in the story. Let Jesus meet you there. This can become a true spiritual encounter with the Lord.

Choose a Scripture from one of these and follow the five prayer steps below: (Pay attention to which Scripture stirs your heart to *want* to do.) Do more than one if you want. Or, be free to choose any Scripture you might want that may not be listed here.

Mark 5:21-34 (healing by touching Jesus' hem)
Mark 5:34 (raising a young girl back to life)
Mark 6:1-6 (in Jesus' home town)
Luke 7:36-50 (Mary Magdalene anoints Jesus' feet)
Luke 13:31-34 (Jesus speaks to Pharisees/agonizes
    over Jerusalem)
John 13:3-17 (Jesus washes the disciples' feet)
John 21:1-25 (on the shore after the resurrection)
Song of Solomon 1:2 (let Him kiss me . . .)
Song of Solomon 2:4-6 (He brought me to His banqueting
    house . . .)

A) <u>Begin by praying</u> that the Lord will guide and be with you during this time of prayer. In faith, be present to Him. Read the Scripture slowly, paying attention to detail. If you wish, read some of the text before and/or after the story to get it into the right context.

B) <u>Meditate</u>: Close your eyes and picture what you've read by becoming part of the story. Allow it to flow with a life of its own.

   Suggestions: Imagine being part of the scene. Be a disciple, or someone healed, a fictional character who meets Jesus, or yourself time/space traveling. Use your imagination. Be creative. Use your five senses to experience it. Hear the sounds, smell the smells, feel the wind. Look at Jesus closely, examine the expressions on His face, His tone of voice, His clothing, the look in His eyes. Listen to His words. Continue until it ends.

C) <u>Dialogue</u>: Write in your journal, describing what happened during the meditation time. Be expectant. This is also a time to communicate with Him, being open and sensitive to His thoughts, words, or feelings.

D) <u>Contemplate</u>: Sit in silence, still within and without, attentive, aware of God's presence. Simply *be* with the Lord. Keep your mind on Him alone. If your mind wanders, bring it back with a single word, "Jesus." Let your love flow back and forth. Sometimes there may be more dialogue, a vision, sense of love, faith, joy, and peace, etc. Be open to whatever the Lord desires. Silence with nothing (seemingly) happening is authentic contemplative prayer.

E) <u>Journal Writing</u>: Document your experience. Sometimes writing to reflect on the experience can be more helpful and enlightening than the time in meditation itself. Keep your "ear" open while writing. Often the Lord will speak more, even as you write. This enriches the experience and you will always have it to review and remember.

Chapter Five

THE PEARL OF PEARLS

*M*ary of Bethany. How Jesus appreciated her. Out of the treasure of her heart, she adorned and anointed our King. Mary had discovered the Pearl of pearls. She sold all to own it. Her portion in life, her greatest and only treasure, became Jesus. Mary discovered the Treasure of all treasures.

This is My favorite chapter. Ah, may I speak a few words through this Christian writer? I interrupted. But then, I'd just like to say, that I might also interrupt your reading. This is a great opportunity, you know. Sometimes speaking in the first person just seems somehow more personal. Did you smile? Maybe your lips didn't, but I know your heart did.

Reading a book about Me means that you want to know Me. I know it's your way of looking for Me. Do you believe Me now? Put the book down a minute and look at Me if you do.

Of course you believe in the incarnation.

Your heart says, "Yes, yes, Lord, I believe You have come down from heaven. You became a man, died, was raised from the dead, and will come again. Yes, yes, Lord, I believe that you have sent your Holy Spirit to me and that You abide in me."

Yes, you do believe in the incarnation. You believe that I am the Good Shepherd who speaks to My sheep, who hear My voice and know Me. You believe that I am the Vine and you are a branch and that you abide in Me. You believe in some great mysteries. I appreciate all of this. Believing in all these things is for a purpose. You are supposed to be progressing. Where? I'll tell you. To Me! I Am. Even right now.

Spelled out, I am in the writer's output (words), I am in the reader's input (words), I am the Word of God. You know, I am speaking to you all the time. All the time! I speak in creation. In events. In silence. In all of life. I speak more without words. Sometimes words themselves get in My way. They so often are inefficient to express My thoughts, My heart, My deepest meanings, Myself. My thoughts are translated into your own words. I speak to babies, animals, the earth and heavens. I certainly don't need words. But I like them. Have you ever thought about what thought is? My Presence is more than communication. Communication is expression of truth and reality. What is truth and reality? I Am. I am personal and I am a Person. I love and I am Love. Do you believe in the incarnation? Please read on.

Mary wasn't a writer. She never wrote a word of Scripture. She wasn't a leader, or teacher of the Church, and she seems to disappear from all historical accounts after her last encounter with Jesus at the dinner not long before His crucifixion. Yet she taught, by far, one of the greatest lessons in the Bible. Jesus said she would be historically remembered. Because she did something He wanted everyone who would hear the Gospel to know. This was of utmost priority. She taught us how to love God. She would be the first of many who would learn loving devotion for our Lord Jesus Christ, the Great Bridegroom.

Oh, tell them about how much I loved them all while in Israel.

His loving us now began with Israel, even in the early days. And, no less today—He still loves Israel. We are a part of His love for Israel, both physical Israel—so much a part of our world news today—and spiritual Israel, whose children we all are. This is mystical.

Now understand, you have all been in My heart ever since I first chose Israel. My promises are for My Bride. She, you—are (all together) My Bride. I have longed for Israel, and you, to know and love Me. I have labored throughout the ages to reveal who I am. All of history holds this revelation.

More personal words can sometimes be found in-between the lines while reading. We are living in-between the lines of God's prophetic plan—in-between Jesus' first coming and His promised return. In His coming to us He speaks of His great, great love. Devotion and intimacy with Jesus cannot happen from past or future experience, but only in the now. Linger here, and let your faith arise. Listen, in-between the lines. It's a good idea to put the book aside and pray whenever your heart feels stirred. Stay in *listening* attentiveness while you read and pray. The Spirit's voice is very gentle, so subtle, that unless you keep a listening ear tuned, you may not notice Him. If you are expectant, you may hear. He meets us in our faith.

God came. Jesus was God's love walking and talking. Mary of Bethany recognized that "something" about Jesus that was so magnetic. He drew her to Himself as only God can do. She welcomed His love without question or doubt. She didn't understand everything about Him but only knew she loved Him. That was enough to know. That was everything.

Once again, Jesus had come to stay with His good friends in Bethany. This time, they were having dinner at Simon's house, who had been a leper. He wasn't a leper anymore, though. Lazarus was there, too, having been recently raised from the dead.

What a dinner. A healed leper and a raised dead man hosting a banquet in honor of their rescuer: their good friend, Jesus. How could anyone act normally around a man with such power? Mary didn't.

Precious memories and love for Jesus filled her heart. He stayed at their home sometimes when He came to Jerusalem. She'd gotten to know Him well. She treasured His words, His inspiring and uplifting stories, and their times of shared experiences. She saw His purity, His humility, and fervor for His mission. She loved His laughter whenever it filled the house. She saw His patience during times of conflict. She loved to listen to Him teach. Mostly, she saw His love. It was magnetic. She seemed to melt into the kindness in His eyes. She felt the depth of His intense personality, sometimes trembling with a holy awe, which mixed with a deep sense of well-being. She felt something akin to security from a powerful authority that emanated from Him. He spoke with wisdom and authority that went beyond comprehension. She trusted and believed in Him. She adored Him. He had given her faith in God. A precious gift.

How did she come to this? It was a process—a revelation over time and events. More and more, love for Jesus grew.

I wasn't teaching or performing miracles that night. I was beginning to feel jittery, too. The time was drawing so close at hand now. I had been staying out of public, way out in remote areas, waiting. I had to stay away to avoid trouble with My enemies before the right time—Passover. The time had come. It was My time.

Jerusalem, and its surrounding vicinities, were swelling with the faithful once again. During the beginning of the week's feast, a dinner was given to honor Me. It was a party. I really appreciated all their thoughts and efforts to please Me. It was so good to be with My friends, My disciples, and some relatives, for a celebration. It really was quite a feast. Lazarus and Simon were being celebrated there, too. One had been dead, the other had wished it because of his leprosy. And yet, I was the only one with death on the mind that evening. Dying, as both Lazarus and Simon know, is not something one wants to do. It's something one must do. That included Me.

I couldn't hide My mood from Mary. A few times I noticed her staring at Me. She kept catching Me with my thoughts showing. I'm not a pretender. She knew something was troubling Me. The troubling thoughts came like waves over Me. I was happy, so very happy, most of the time. I was so much enjoying everyone. I felt good and ready for the most part. It's just the whole terrible ordeal ahead of Me was not something I could easily stop thinking about. It was always there. I was living one day at a time, knowing it would be over soon.

They didn't know it was a farewell party. I was saying good-bye to them in My own subtle ways, each one so dear. I wanted them all to have special memories. I said something to Mary about how much I appreciated her. She asked Lazarus privately if he knew what was wrong with Me, but he told her to ask herself.

Her question was, "Lord, what will happen to You in Jerusalem?" Her question was her own answer. She knew enough in her spirit. I didn't need to tell her. I told her I would always be with her.

His words reminded her of the ones He had said to Martha. How can He say He will always be with me? What does that mean if not simply what He says? Before, when He said, "I am the Resurrection and the Life," He immediately raised her brother from the dead. His words always performed the deeds.

Watching Him those hours during the party, recent memories of Lazarus' death and resurrection played in Mary's mind so vividly.

She had sunk into the darkness of despair that terrible week as she daily watched her brother die. To add to that pain, she and Martha also felt abandoned by Jesus because He had not come to help them, when He had helped so many others, so many strangers. Is this how to treat friends?

All week Mary had prayed almost unceasingly, often leaving her brother's bedside to stand at the gate looking down the path that led to their house, anxious for the first glimpse of Jesus. Because Jesus and Lazarus were such close friends, she knew He would come regardless of the danger. It was well known that Jesus' life was in jeopardy. For that reason, He and His disciples had been staying in remote areas. Knowing where He was, they had sent a messenger to tell Him of Lazarus' grave condition. But the messenger returned and days went by claiming the life of Lazarus. Heartache, loss, and grief were the answers to Mary's prayers. Jesus had not come.

Mary remembered how she had felt when she first saw Jesus four days after her brother's death. Her emotions were like a hurricane. She was grieved by her brother's loss and stricken with disappointment in the One she adored. But upon seeing Him, she was overjoyed because He had finally come.

No one was posted at the gate anymore. Some children had seen Jesus walking in the direction of their home and ran ahead with the news. Martha was told and ran out to greet Him. Mary stayed inside, reluctant to face Him. Later, Martha told Mary of the amazing conversation they had as the two of them stood together on the steep path leading up to their property. At the time, Martha thought His words had symbolic meaning. They were, in reality, among the boldest claims He'd ever made. He said to her, "Martha, your brother will live again . . . I am the resurrection and the life. . . . He who believes in Me will never die. . . . Do you believe this? . . . Martha, go get Mary."

Jesus had a wonderful gift He could hardly wait to give. He couldn't even wait to go up and greet her at the house. He sent for her. Mary's love brought her running to Him. Falling at His feet, she chided Him. "How could You, Jesus, how could You do this to us? You did not come to help us. Lazarus is dead. You are too late now."

But He already knew her pain, the loss, the mixed thoughts, and the disappointment. It was her weeping that really got to Him. It opened His emotional floodgates. He didn't speak a word. His compassion spoke volumes as He joined Mary's tears with His own and lifted her to her feet for a strong embrace.

How many know the sorrows of a crying God? The sorrows of the earth fall like torrents from My eyes. Mary's heartache gripped Me so fast and hard. My heart broke in union with hers. It brings Me great pain when My beloveds hurt. I share in it deeply. Always. Every pain, disappointment, and frustration. I am an emotional God. You have been made in My image. You cry like I do. You laugh and dance when your spirit so moves you. It happens when My Spirit moves you too. Beloved, when you cry, if I abide in you and you abide in Me, whose tears are whose? Do you believe in the incarnation?

Jesus took Mary's head in His hands, and looking into uplifted face, into teary eyes, said, "Come, show Me where you have laid him." When they arrived there, He pointed at the large stone which blocked the opening of the tomb and said He wanted it rolled out of the way. It was a large flat rolling stone that moved along a chiseled-out groove in front of the cave's entrance. It was the same type of stone that would cover the grave of *His own* resurrection.

When Martha saw what Jesus intended, she tried to stop Him. She reasoned with Him that the smell would be too terrible. "Jesus," she thought, "You're four days too late."

"Martha, didn't you hear what I said back there? If you believe, you will see the glory of God."

The stone was removed.

He had raised others . . . But four days! . . . even His own disciples stood in disbelief. The grievers and Jesus' traveling companions made up an audience which now silently stood around the cemetery, all eyes were fixed on the Man kneeling in front of an open cave-like grave.

Jesus raised His eyes to heaven and prayed out loud to His Father. He thanked His Father for what He was about to do. He prayed for the sakes of those standing around Him—that this miracle would help them have faith in Him—for eternal life.

Mary stood close to John and Martha, her eyes glued to Jesus. Is this really happening? What is He attempting to do? Hope and faith were rising up within her—she was believing the impossible.

After He finished praying, He stood and moved to the entrance of the tomb. He bent and peered into it. There was a narrow entrance and a couple of stairs leading down into a little room dug out of the side of the limestone hill. Down hidden in the darkness of the tomb was a slab of smooth flat rock, and upon it lay the still body of Lazarus wrapped in a shroud and strips of linen. Jesus felt the presence of death and Satan. His thoughts envisioned His own dark grave awaiting Him. Then, in a loud voice, the commanding words of Life exploded into the darkness: "Lazarus, come out!" Jesus backed up and stood a few yards from the opening of the cave to await Lazarus. Lazarus immediately stirred and made his way out. When he emerged out from the dark hole into the bright afternoon sun, his white wrappings glared a brilliance that added even more awe to the onlookers. He looked like a dazzling ghost up from the darkness of death. He was no ghost and certainly not a corpse. It was Lazarus. Jesus got just what He asked for. His word was creative power.

Little lamb, have you noticed when I say something it has the power of creation? For example, if I say to you, "Have confidence." You will have confidence. Or, if I say, "Forgive so and so," you can forgive because I impart the power and ability to do it. When I said, "Let there be light," the light didn't think about appearing or even hesitate. It simply was. When I speak to you, however, you always have a choice to make. Often that

*choice hinges upon whether you believe, accept, or want it. When
I said, "Lazarus, come forth!" Only Lazarus came up from that
grave. He heard and responded to My voice. Life and love
creatively, powerfully, calls each one personally. Do you hear?*

Lazarus emerged from the dark cave laughing uproariously,
praising God. He couldn't wait to get freed from the wrappings
and was trying his best to squirm out of them. Jesus called to
a couple of men to quickly unbind him. Three of the disciples
ran to help. Jesus turned and found Mary quickly with His
eyes. He smiled. She was in blissful shock. He brought her
brother, Lazarus, up out of a grave of four days. While Jesus
looked at her, she fell to her knees. Then Jesus turned back to
face Lazarus with the warmest, most loving smile still lingering.

Mass hysteria reigned. The cheering crowd of people jumping
and dancing praised God. Some stood still in disbelief or awe.
One person fainted. A few ran to Jerusalem with the news.

Still kneeling, Mary watched the two favorite men in her
life. While Lazarus' bindings were being unwound, she couldn't
see Jesus' face because His back was toward her. He hadn't
changed His position where He stood since Lazarus had come
out of the cave. The look on Lazarus' face she would never
forget. His laughing had turned to joyful weeping. He looked
at Jesus with love and worship. After a while, still beholding
each other, a gentle, knowing smile spread across Lazarus' face.
Both of them were crying now; Mary watched Jesus wipe His
own tears away as He went to Lazarus and then kissed him on
both cheeks. Lazarus returned the holy kiss of greeting. Jesus
began to laugh with great joy, as did Lazarus and many others.
Jesus took His friend by the arm and they started for the house.
He motioned to Mary and the others to come along with them.
They were followed by His marveling disciples and a whole crowd
of new-found followers. Mary walked beside them, awestruck.
Overwhelmed.

Lazarus was alive! And Jesus was back. Her close and
beloved friend, Jesus. Her mind couldn't grasp the impact of
this momentous event, not fully. It was incomprehensible.

Jesus had taken the initiative to reveal Himself to Mary
and all the others involved in that experience at Bethany.

Jesus had to leave the area and go to the desert village of Ephraim for awhile after that. It was even more dangerous for Him now since this miracle. Jesus' enemies were positive His death was the only sure answer to this "Nazarene Matter." Earlier that year the high priest had prophesied that this man's death would save the nation of Israel and, through it, all the world. They thought they would be doing God a great service to kill Jesus. Yes, it was God's plan. Jesus would return to Jerusalem in time to be the Passover Lamb.

Jesus was popular with most of the people. This is why His enemies had to capture Him in secret. Thousands of Jewish pilgrims converged in Jerusalem and were anxious to see Him, hoping He would be brave enough to come for the week of Passover. Anyone who saw Him was supposed to report this to the Sanhedrin. And anyone who "followed" Him was banned from the Temple grounds.

When He appeared on the outskirts of the holy city, a little beyond Bethany, thousands of Jewish pilgrims exuberantly proclaimed Him as their Messianic King. They dramatically and formally ushered Him in through Jerusalem's gates with a large procession, waving palms, and singing praises. The praises were long held to be Psalms for the coming King—the Messiah. The gentle king came into His city. But there would be no crown. The religious authorities had other plans. Soon after the procession, Jesus cleared out the temple a second time, adding fuel to the wildfire of envy and hate burning in His enemies' minds.

Jesus spent some nights during that last week with faithful friends in Bethany. One night they had a special dinner for Him at Simon's house. The women, including Martha and Mary, brought food and enjoyed the festive celebration. They were celebrating life! Mary sensed something different in Jesus. Often, He could be quite serious, but this was not the same. It wasn't anything He said. It was in His eyes, the tone of voice, and the quiet reserve she sensed in Him. Maybe all those hassles from the authorities were weighing on Him.

What was the secret? What terrible thing was Jesus facing? She looked at her brother, so full of life again. Jesus could do anything. And yet He had lingered and let Lazarus die. Why did He do that? Then came that glorious day when He said to

Martha, "I am the Resurrection and the Life." She reflected on how Jesus often said "Believe in Me." It was becoming easy to believe in Him. Jesus was so much more than His message. Believing in the Teacher was so much more important than just His teaching. He did impossible things—signs and wonders, miracles, healings, and resurrections followed Him like a trail. Yes, she believed in *Him*.

As she pondered these thoughts, Mary observed Jesus and Lazarus reclining near each other. They were such close friends. Outwardly, Jesus seemed to be appreciating this time a great deal. He had lovingly gazed at individuals throughout the evening, including herself. He wasn't teaching or sharing stories. He was simply there with them. Several times the conversation took on serious tones as the men discussed the political situation, but Jesus said very little about it. Everyone seemed jovial and upbeat. This night filled them—especially His disciples—with optimism. All were having a good time and were joking, laughing, and feasting.

Jesus was glad for this evening, surrounded with good friends. But increasing dread also visited Him—the ordeal was this week. The next couple of days were all He had left. He had taught and prepared His disciples for all that they could bear for now. Although, He knew there was so much more He wanted to tell them. He'd have to do a lot of talking in the next couple of days . . . But, tomorrow, He'd spend time alone to pray. It wasn't easy finding solitude around Jerusalem during the feasts—the whole area filled with pilgrims, and many stayed in tents almost anywhere where flat ground could be found. Some of His family stayed with Elizabeth during the feasts. She lived in Ein Karem which wasn't conveniently close, but Jesus knew of some shepherds' caves near her house. He'd pray and then visit with His family—one last time. That visit wouldn't be easy. But right now, He put it out of His mind to enjoy this special night with His friends. He was thankful for it.

Mary wanted to do something to honor Jesus—the evening was to honor Him, after all. She didn't understand it, but somehow the God of Israel and Jesus connected, and she wanted nothing in life but Him! She had thought of just the right thing that would appropriately show her love to the Messiah. The idea to anoint Him came with sheer delight.

Perhaps God the Father had given birth to the idea. It was perfect for her. Her love was the reason. She couldn't wait. She had an alabaster jar of very expensive spikenard, a rare, perfumed oil, from the East Indies. The fragrance of which could only begin to express the sweet intoxication—adoration—she felt for Jesus. The liquid treasure was her most valuable possession. How could she better show Him her love? This act would say more than words ever could.

She brought it from home, but waited until after the meal was over. Taking the alabaster jar from within a pocket in the folds of her garment, she slowly approached Jesus. She knelt next to Him as He reclined on large pillows, positioned at the short end of the horseshoe-shaped table. Lazarus was on the other side of Him. She knelt between Simon and Jesus, broke the jar's seal and began pouring before He fully realized she was even there. The airy lavender-like odor permeated the whole house and the drama unfolded before all present. The entire room became voiceless except for a few initial gasps. Everyone knew this extravagance was unreasonable, yet Jesus did nothing to stop her. Most were more surprised by Jesus' non-action than Mary's actions.

She poured slowly, starting with the top of His head. The liquid trickled down His scalp, under and into His clothes, then further onto the pillow on which He leaned. A little of it trickled down His forehead and He closed His eyes as she brushed the stream away. It was a whole pint. She then went to rubbing His head, working the rich oils into His hair. Caressing His temples and beard with the oil, she anointed Him, not only with the oil, but with her love. Having saved some, she walked around to His feet, sat down on the floor and gently lifted them into her lap where she proceeded to rub more of the oil, not a small amount, into His calloused, bare feet. Eventually, she wiped the excess off with her long, silky hair. The jar was completely empty. She lifted the vase and shook it upside down to show Jesus it was all gone, and then went back to rubbing His feet. Jesus laughed warmly, affectionately, with her.

But before she'd gone to His feet, Jesus had felt most enraptured by the entire experience. He felt the warm, tenderness of her fingers. He'd been quite taken, captivated, by this very intimate human display of affection. When she first started, He froze perfectly still, in silent cooperation, while she did what she wanted.

Oh, this is divine, He thought to Himself. His eyes filled with tears and the two held one another's gaze a few moments.

Later, these precious moments of adoration would often fill up her heart when she remembered the way His eyes locked with hers. Neither of them spoke a word. In silence, love was expressed.

Prophets, priests, and kings had been anointed before. But, this this was love's anointing. This act of appreciation so due His Majesty, became the first act of devotion His Bride, the Church, would show Him. Mary couldn't have realized the impact it would later have as so many of His loving followers have, spiritually, followed her example. But it was the beginning of something very beautiful, very right, and very satisfying—for both of them.

Before she finished, some of the men started to complain about the waste, saying that it could have been sold and the money used for the poor. After all, as Judas had truthfully pointed out, it was worth a full year's wages. In their eyes, it was all foolishly wasted. Jesus ignored the rebuke at first, too absorbed in watching Mary rubbing His feet. When she heard Judas' words and worriedly looked up at Jesus for His response, He resolutely turned to face Judas and swiftly scanned the entire room with His eyes. "Leave her alone. Why are you bothering her? She has done a beautiful thing to Me." He looked back at Mary with a tender smile, holding her eyes steadily with His own. His face communicated to her the message of appreciation and love. After a couple moments, He stood and looked from one to another in the room: "The poor you will always have with you, and you can help them any time you want. But you will not always have Me. She did what she could. She poured this fragrant ointment on My body to prepare Me for burial. I tell you the truth, wherever the gospel is preached throughout the world, what she has done will also be told, in memory of her." Once again, Jesus was defending her for her devotion. Once again, He told His disciples the reality: He was about to die. It just didn't fit in with their ideas about the Messiah, whom they'd come to believe Him to be.

She was numb from His attention, yet His words confirming His death and the fact that she anointed His body for burial pierced her heart. She was so glad she had given Him this gift of devotion.

The Messiah (Anointed One) certainly was anointed by the Holy Spirit in the works that He did. Historically, God saw to it that a king, especially, was anointed with oil before beginning his mission and reign. A prophet usually would do this. But the only prophet at this time was Jesus. Except for Mary. She prophesied without words. She formally anointed the Anointed One. It was a sign from God the Father for the Savior to receive His mission orders. Through this extravagant act of devotion, Mary was the "Samuel" appointed by God to pour the symbolic oil upon the chosen "David," King. This anointing formally commissioned Jesus for His special mission. Also, in traditional terms, this anointing prepared His body for burial. But, the significance here is Mary's love. Her love anointed Him, too. And, after all, that is why He came to save. That is why He came to die and rise again: to enable us to love Him once again. For mankind hadn't intimately known and loved Him since the Fall. The sweet smell of spikenard oil lingered on both of them those next terrible days. Both of them had it in their hair. Its constant scent during those tortuous hours also may have given Him sweet incentive to endure His sufferings.

Yes, Mary wasted much on Jesus. For love she acted the fool. She wasted her most precious and valuable possession on Him. Gladly. Oh, that we might all become so foolish—and so wise. So poor, for His sake, and so rich. She showed us how to love Him.

She took fragrant oil and anointed the One who created smell. The One who created the plants from which the rich oils came. The One who made her hands, with which to hold the precious ointment. The One who formed the heart and emotions with which to love. The one who sat before her—mostly unrecognized for who He really was—this One was ready to pour out His life completely. He was the extravagantly "wasteful" One—the One who is always ready to pour out His divine life upon all those who desire Him.

When we anoint Jesus and show Him our love and affection today, we often find it happens in a variety of ways. In our prayer life and our various ways of worship we give love to Him. We give the best of ourselves to others for His sake. In all these ways, Jesus is present. We are in Him and He is in us. That's what the incarnation is about today. How many recognized the mystery of the incarnation when God in Jesus physically walked on the earth? How many recognized the face of God when they saw Him? Who could grasp who He really was? Ironically, it's still like that today. Often, we don't recognize Him in the most obvious places.

"I won't leave you as orphans," Jesus said, "I will come to you . . . And will abide in you and you in Me." If we Christians had the faith to fully grasp that and allow it to be lived out, our world would be a much different place. What a radical difference the Church would make. Immanuel—God with us—has come to transform us into His image. Jesus brings us to know ourselves. From Him we learn *who* we are, and *why* we are.

Without God's divine grace and love we wouldn't even think about Him. He is the initiator of our relationship with Him. Our desire for God comes from Him. He loves us first. He draws each of us to Himself.

We are each a reflection of God—a painting on His canvas. A song He is singing. Our days and experiences are the dance He is dancing. His own glory can be seen in the reflection of God in our lives.

Jesus lived His life most fully. And now all of His own are filled with His life. We are His reflection. More, we are His gentle and willing hands; swift and persistent feet; strong and loving arms; kind and healing lips; and hopeful, love-filled eyes. We can *be* Jesus to others, and others can *be* Jesus to us. God will always remain the *Other.* We will always love and worship Him above all else. Jesus prayed to the Father: ". . . That they all may be one, as You, Father, are in Me, and I in You; that they also may be one in Us, that the world may believe that You sent Me." (John 17:21) This is life in union with God and this is the incarnation.

Prayer Journal Exercises:

1. This might feel like a silly thing to do, but if you would partake in a little "foolishness" for heaven's sake (sorry for the pun), there could be a little gift in it for you from God. Go look in the mirror, and when you see yourself reflected there, say a little prayer. "Lord, is that You in me?" This is just a little visual lesson to say that we do most certainly reflect the Lord and so delight His heart.

    Now that you're back from the mirror, behold His glory in the reflection of God in your own life. Take a few minutes to journal about your gifts (all He's given you, both natural and spiritual). Make a list of them—your natural abilities and skills, your strengths and your spiritual graces. Ask God to help you see these things. Prayerfully ask: Who am I? Why do I do what I do? See yourself through Love's eyes. God's eyes. Think about what you really love to do: your creative passions, etc. Music, writing, gardening, being a good friend? St. Augustine once said, "Love God with all your heart, then do whatever you will." You see, if you love God, your desires and His become one and the same.

2. We all often hear that condemning, critical voice within—it is the accuser of the saints. We often respond to God's love with "What about my sinfulness?" (The concern of "not ever being able to measure up" problem.) But, hear God's answer: *"What about My grace?"* When we do well we get this: "What about my motives? I never seem to do things right. Even if I do, my motives so often trip me up." (That Romans 7:17 syndrome.) Now, listen to this! *"What about My love? My love covers you, My beloved, faithful one. All I ask of you is faith and obedience. My own goodness has saved you. My goodness I freely give you. Just take it. You are becoming perfect. You are becoming the real you! You are (being) fearfully and wonderfully re-made."* (The process of sanctification.) Here's a poem just for you.

You

I had a thought;
It was you.
I dreamed you, desired you . . .
O, everything about you!

I took My time
Contemplating how you'd be Mine.
That special one-of-a-kind
Whose life would dance
and shine.

I dreamed a lot;
And weaved you together
of all loving thoughts.
Thrilled with the good
that I sought
All for you.

O, My precious,
My work of art
I've loved you, desired you,
right from the start

Stories I told you;
beauty to astound you;
grace to clothe you;
jealous, I woo you.

I'm always near you, loving you,
so very nigh.
Like a bird to fly, or a fish swim,
you were made for love,
and to be Mine

Have you seen the mountains?
That's how proud I am of you.
Climb one with Me and you'll see;
or, believe for one to go into the sea.
I'll do it for you. How I love you.

I just had to show you My love,
you know.
My heart, My tears, My blood,
My pain.
You're won by the love
of the One you'll gain.

I know life hurts,
it hurt Me too.
But believe what I tell you
that I really do love you.
Believe Me.
That's all I want you to do,
and if you do,
then one day, you'll know
all that I know
about you.

3. Prayerfully read Psalm 139. Let God personally speak to you about how He feels about you. Treat this as a question Jesus is asking: "What do you think I love the most about you?" Have you heard His nickname for you? Be open and expectant if you haven't.

4. Song of Solomon 2:4 says: *"He brought me to His banqueting house, and His banner over me was love."* Think about what the word "banner" means. Think about how banners have been used in the past and how we use them in modern times. Banners are wonderful to see in churches—they make worshipful statements about who God is. If you could design and make a banner for God, what would it look like? Before you do this, think about what you love the most about God. What are your favorite images of God? (Good Shepherd, Father, Bridegroom, Divine Friend, Rock, Savior, King of Kings, Healer.) These images are how God has revealed Himself to you. What image of Him draws you, one that you haven't yet experienced? (This is where He may be leading you next.)

    Picture Jesus coming to visit you. A band of angels arrive and stand around you. Imagine them stepping aside as Jesus passes from the rear and moves up to the front of them to stand before of you. He is holding up a banner. He has come to personally give it to you. Something is written on it. This banner is a sign He desires to give you so that you will understand a precious truth about you, your unique giftedness, or perhaps your "life's mission statement." Maybe it is a truth about Himself. What does your banner say? What is He wanting to impart to you? What authority is being given? What truth will you begin to walk in and understand? Can you draw a picture of it? Perhaps it's an image like a cross, or a lamb, or words, or a name. As you "see" it do you wish to take this banner from Him? Will you carry it for Him? Pay attention to the divine whispers—turn them into banners that shout truth into your life.

Chapter Six

THE GARDENS OF THE LORD

The First Garden ~

At the time when God created the heavens and the earth, there was a beautiful, exclusive place He made on the earth. It was delightful. Designed with much thought and care, it has been called Paradise because it was a heavenly place of bliss. But it wasn't an elaborate place with golden streets, or a sea of crystal with gates of pearls, nor were glory and light shining from it, as heaven itself is described. Nor was it awesome in majesty as some mountains and valleys are in other parts of the earth. It had no massive and powerful ocean, no windswept desert landscapes, no breathtaking waterfalls from heights of the earth. Rather, it had an enclosed and private feeling to it because this special place was made with a distinct purpose in mind.

It was a garden. God named it "the Garden of Eden," which means "delight." And that was its intent. What made it so delightful was the love and friendship found in it.

The great decorator designed and planted it Himself. It was beautiful, teeming with life so green, full of trees and colorful flowers. It had gentle brooks running over rocks, chirping birds, singing creatures, soft velvet carpeted grass, hidden coves under veils of ferns and vines, and gentle breezes carrying aromatic scents. It was all very pleasant and peaceful.

The great artist designed the universe, giving the earth most special regard. He formed it with awesome variations and beauty. His wisdom established order. His delight in beauty was expressed. It pleased Him to create a universe within a single cell and worlds within a universe. Components of matter and energy, living cells, genetic formulae gave expression to His thoughts. All of these things were a part of the Creator's masterpiece and was found in this wonderful garden. Here was the beginning of all His dreams.

Within this garden, the Creator planted trees and plants bearing fruit and provided water and sunshine—everything that was needed to sustain natural life. The Creator first prepared everything, readying the garden to be a life-sustaining environment; then He filled the garden with living creatures. Interestingly, they all had mates—male and female. In fact, He intended that all created life—mammal, bird, fish, insect, and plant—would reproduce, each kind producing like kind.

Isn't it true that an artist is expressed by His work? Life and love. That is the essense of God's being. The Creator was full of love, and the essence of love is *to give*. He made beings to love which, because of the nature of love, might love in return. He also realized that love must be free, just as He was free. So, He placed at the garden's center two special trees. They were the "Tree of Life", which bore the fruit of eternal life, and the "Tree of the Knowledge of Good and Evil", which bore the fruit of death. The second was absolutely forbidden with the warning that its fruit would cause death.

He had made other eternal beings besides these. Thousands of angels. But at least one-third of them had rebelled against Him. One result was that evil had entered the dominions of God's kingdom.

He had made Adam in His own likeness. The Creator had breathed His own life—His Spirit—into this newly created being and placed him in the garden. They became close companions. Adam was not like the other earthly creatures God had made, because he was alone, without a mate. Like God. Adam was made in God's image. But God saw that all was not good in this regard. Adam should have a mate.

Romantic love. There is nothing more delightful than being in love. If a male and a female have love that is pure, and if they can be together, there is no finer thing on earth. It can be passionate and stronger than death. This kind of love is sweeter than the love between parents and children. It is better than the love between siblings. It is more precious than the love between good friends. It is the best love. Truly, it is the wine of Life.

God's love can be all these kinds of relational love. He loves with unconditional, sacrificial love. He loves as a perfect parent who loves His children. He loves as a brother through Jesus' human connection with us. He loves as a friend who sticks closer than a brother. And, with the strongest and best of all types of love, He loves as a lover in the fullest sense. That's why He has revealed Himself as our Bridegroom. It was His idea, not ours.

He wanted to be in love. He wanted "another" to love. Just like Adam wanted one. God, who created love, who is love, will not miss out. This special kind of love exists for His sake as well as ours. However, human "eros" love is but a shadow compared to the original. Who could have known those early days in the first garden that God had a long-range plan? Even in the beginning, He knew how Adam would feel and did feel. He had planned to give Adam a mate all along. A part of Adam would be missing, but it would be in Eve. God put Adam in a deep sleep and opened his side, removing one of his ribs. From it He formed Eve, his counterpart, who became Adam's beautiful mate. She was very much like him, but almost opposite in some ways. She was smaller, softer, weaker in a delicate, fragile sort of way, very sensitive, and extremely lovely.

Likewise, God's bride would be formed from Himself, as Eve was formed from Adam. The Creator's mate would be formed from Spirit, and she would resemble Eve in similar ways. Flesh gives birth to flesh, but Spirit gives birth to spirit.

God loved the man and woman—humankind—so much. They loved Him, and they loved each other, too. This greatly pleased the Lord. And the Lord watched them together, and He dreamed.

One day Adam and Eve ate from the forbidden fruit of the tree of the knowledge of good and evil. The tempter told them they would know everything just like God. But after disobeying God, the next thing they realized was that they were naked. God found them hiding from Him as they tried covering themselves. So God covered their shame with the skins of an animal. It marked the beginning of blood being sacrificed to cover humankind's sin. This, God knew would only cover the shame; one day He would remove the shame. That day would prove His love and faithfulness to them. That day He would enter into death Himself and awake from it, swallowing up death with His Life. No longer could anyone die if His Life was in them. And like Adam, who was put into a deep sleep while Eve was formed from Him, so, too, God would be put into a "death/ sleep" so that His bride could be formed from Him, made from His very nature and being. This was His future plan and the only thing that could comfort Him that sad day when sin and death came to His beloved Adam and Eve.

He knew all the pain, suffering, sickness, sin, evil—even murder—which would follow them and their children. And He knew they would not know Him intimately, nor live in harmony with Him, as they had. Though His heart was full of pain, He gave the orders. They were forcefully taken out of the garden. An angel was commissioned with a heavenly weapon, a sword of fire, to guard the entrance. They were not allowed near the Tree of Life anymore. They couldn't come back into this garden— not for a long, long, time.

He comforted Himself in that He had plans to make good come from all of this. But it wouldn't be easy. It would cost Him dearly. The cross was in full view. In fact, it was part of His plan. It would be love at its best, and hate at its worst. But to display love at its best, He decided it would be worth it.

He wanted a mate—a counterpart. Mostly, He wanted to be a lover. He wanted to be married. Yes, after it was all over, it would be worth it.

He could see His bride even now. Yet she was way off in the distance, in His mind's eye. She was beautiful, so pure and holy, like Him. She would love Him completely. He would provide her with elegant robes of righteousness and adorn her with precious, rare jewels. Not earthly ones. These would be spiritual: refined, polished and valuable gems. He would forever cherish her, would lay down His life for her—how much He would love her! She would be His beloved companion and mate forever. And she would rule with Him, right beside Him. They would be happy and fulfilled, gracefully complementing one another. They would content each other's hearts. She belonged to Him with abandon, enraptured by His love, and He possessed Her with the fire of consuming passion. Divine fires of love would blaze between them for eternity.

A Garden in the Land of Israel ~

*J*esus went to the garden one last time. It was the Garden of Gethsemane, just outside the walls of Jerusalem. This garden was very special because it was close to Mount Moriah, the most sacred place on the earth, where stood the holy temple of God. This holy ground, chosen by God, was a place of faith, starting with Abraham and ending with the New Jerusalem from where the Messiah would reign over all the earth. Appropriately, God saw to it that there was a garden nearby.

Whenever Jesus was in Jerusalem, it was here in this garden, where He often met and communed with His Father. Jesus was thankful for it, remembering the original garden was designed just for this purpose. He liked coming to this garden to get away from the noise and crowds to rest and pray. It was peaceful and private. On warmer nights, He and His disciples slept here under the stars. When cooler, they slept in the cave that offered a large, warm, shelter complete with a spring of water. They all enjoyed the beauty and refreshment of the olive garden. But this visit was different. It wasn't peaceful or restful. And, it wouldn't be private for long. His dreaded hour had arrived. Here, in this garden, He freely gave up His freedom. Here in one of His favorite places to be, He made a choice. Paradoxically, it paralleled the choice Adam and Eve made in the first garden. Jesus, too, chose the fruit from the tree of death. Only His choice was obedience and redeemed their choice of disobedience.

The original plan was coming to a crucial point. He knew what He had to do. But His mind felt cloudy and His heart heavy. This was the agreed price for His bride and without Him she would die.

He asked His three closest friends to come apart from the eight others. These were the three who were usually beside Him. They had seen Jesus transfigured into radiance on top of a mount. They had heard the Father's voice from heaven speak on Jesus' behalf more than twice. They lived and worked together in close company. They knew Him well. But it was difficult seeing Jesus like this. He was acting strangely: weak, even needy. This, together with the puzzling and dramatic Passover meal they'd just experienced with Him, caused them to feel depressed and tired. Slowly, the four of them walked together out of earshot from the rest. But Jesus, in doing so, was releasing the iron guard He'd been wearing all day. Suddenly, the reality of the moment hit Him with full force. This time of waiting became the beginning of His sufferings. Like a woman in labor, His travail had begun. He stopped walking and they all stood together, in a little circle. He wanted to tell them how He felt, but He also wanted to appear strong and sure for their sake, so that their faith in Him would not waver. But His meekness won over, and He revealed His anxiety to them. He put His arms around Peter and John's shoulders and looked across into James' face and confided, "My soul is overwhelmed with sorrow to the point of death." His voice was low and cracking as He fought to maintain composure. He leaned heavily on His disciples, hung His head, and let out a long, painful groan that was mixed with a strangled prayer. They stood for a little while in this circle of bowed heads until Jesus decided they should walk. Joined together in a line, with Jesus in the middle, He continued leaning on Peter and John as they walked deeper into the garden.

His friends felt His body's stiffness and tremor. His breathing was irregular and He was trying to cope with the pain. It wasn't physical pain. It was emotional. Never had He known this kind of weakness. This weakness was far worse than that experienced during His forty-day fast in the desert.

The three didn't know what to say or do for Him. They felt helpless. Jesus realized this. He saw ahead of them a darkened area of the garden, which was surrounded thickly by trees and bushes, blocking out the moon's light. He desired its sheltered darkness. More than anything, He wanted to go and fall into His Father's invisible arms to pray. He realized only His Father could really help Him. As a man, Jesus needed God, but He wanted His friends to stay close, too. "Stay here and keep watch with Me." He walked a few feet away into the darkness, fell prostrate on the ground and cried out to His Father. His agony took the form of long, drawn-out sobs erupting from the depths of His soul.

Hearing their beloved Master wailing was unbearable. Unthinkable. They'd seen Him change water into wine, walk on the sea, still raging storms, wake dead people, command obedience from demons, restore health to thousands of diseased and deteriorating bodies, and transform hardened sinners into holy, loving souls. His words had struck the ears of His hearers like a sword. His claims were always followed by related deeds. Always in charge, He walked in wisdom and power they knew came from heaven. And, they felt secure whenever with Him. So much so, often they mistook their security in Him for bravery. But not right now. Not with Him like this. Their own ears tortured them. Jesus was not acting like Himself. After listening for a while, they laid down close to each other and began to silently pray and think. Their love, confusion, full stomachs, and wine all mixed together had made them drowsy and in denial of reality. Each of them were silent with his own thoughts and torment. They could hear His cries and prayers, and during one stretch of muffled weeping, and then silence, they all fell asleep. While Jesus wept, they slept.

Alone, He fought against hell in the greatest struggle and battle of all time. He was fighting against the chief of all temptations. All hell focused its power in the darkened garden that night—as spiritual enemies tormented the soul of Jesus and lulled His friends to sleep. The devil saw, because of God's love for humankind, that He could be hurt. God was vulnerable. God selflessly loved humankind so much that He'd left Himself wide open to Satan's power. Satan believed he could destroy God because of this weakness. This garden was the Garden of the "oil press", the Aramaic word for Gethsemane, and Life was being pressed down by the forces of hell. Jesus thought of His own recent teaching: "Unless a grain of wheat falls into the earth and dies, it remains alone; but if it dies it bears much fruit." He used that parable aware of its full meaning for Himself and all those who would follow Him. He would be the ultimate example of "dying to self". He had said that if one tried to keep his own life, he would lose it. Jesus felt the weight of responsibility. His life was the first seed, without His there would be no others.

Again, it was Life against death in the garden. The devil had tempted Eve to think of herself as independent of God, to prove it by following her own will and disobeying God's will. Jesus' journey to the cross had started there in the Garden of Eden. It was—and still is—the "self versus God" struggle when these wills cross each other. God Himself had to experience this struggle, this battle, and win it for all humankind. The real "cross" was endured by Jesus, not only on Calvary as He physically hung and suffered unto death, but also here, in this garden, during His inner battle. Jesus, God and human, suffered and died to Himself in the Garden of Gethsemane. He had to lay down His life. It was time now to become a seed. He must die and be planted in the earth. When He would rise again, He would be changed. And from Him would be produced like kind. His bride would be formed from Him, from His own resurrected nature. He knew He had to die. This was something He'd never done before, another new experience since becoming a man. But He knew the full weight of the shame and suffering awaiting Him. He knew He would receive the punishment and judgment for all sin. Details of the crucifixion vexed His imagination in vivid visions. How well He knew the Scriptures: Isaiah 53, Psalm 22, and more. He meditated on Psalm 40:6-8: "Sacrifice and meal offering Thou has not desired; My ears Thou has opened: Burnt offering and sin offering Thou has not required. Then I said, 'Behold, I come; in the scroll of the book it is written of Me; I delight to do Thy will, O my God; Thy law is within my heart.'"

As always, Jesus lived the "cross" in His heart. It was His way of life. He would not disobey His Father. "Father, this body You have prepared for Me is Yours," He prayed.

But Jesus knew His Father, and that anything was possible. Maybe there was another way. Swinging back and forth in His mind He found no peace—reeling between His two choices. He was suffering immensely from the anxiety of it. He thought of His disciples—their confusion and pain. His poor mother—her heart would be stabbed with the knife of love. It was just as the prophet Simeon had predicted when Jesus was a baby in her arms at the temple. Jesus' mother had told Him the story when He was older. Now, He remembered that conversation. Wouldn't this horrible thing be too awful a thing for her to bear? Why? Why does it have to be so? Can't it be some other way? The pain His loved ones were to endure began to overwhelm Him. He had to stop thinking of it.

"Abba!" He cried into the dark, "If it is possible, may this cup be taken from Me?" But then immediately, afraid of being unwilling, He prayed, "Yet not as I will, but as You will."

Is there any other way? Like Isaac, could I, too, be spared? Is there a ram in the thicket for Me? Suddenly, He realized that He was sitting in close geographical proximity as where Isaac's ram had been caught, near Mount Moriah where the temple now stood. I am the ram caught in the thicket—no other will be provided. This is My Father's sacrifice, too. I am also Father's Isaac.

He was the only perfect sacrifice, making it a just and righteous offering for all of humankind's redemption. It had to be His blood, none other, that could merit justification.

It had started in the first garden, the dripping blood on Adam and Eve, as they were given the animal skins to cover their nakedness, no longer innocent. The sacrifice of a life—a life for life—was the only acceptable way. His life alone qualified because He had never sinned, and didn't deserve to die. His life could be a ransom—Life for life. This had been the plan from the very start.

His Father was silent. Jesus could feel the beginning of judgment, the judgment He was to endure for the sake of the world. But He prayed, still hoping for the impossible. Then an angel appeared. Jesus knew immediately that His Father had sent the angel, out of His love, to strengthen Him. But more, the angel's presence meant "No other way."

"I must accept it." He glanced at the angel and then buried His head in His hands. "Yes, yes, I must. Father, help Me. Oh, Abba . . . What will it be like?" He prayed earnestly in such anxiety that His sweat became beads of blood all over His body. His tunic began to cling to Him and His hair felt wet and sticky. He could smell the blood, and was nauseated. But His will was stronger than His senses. Usually a person would short-circuit into unconsciousness when the body could bear no more, but He was a strong and healthy man. This made His agony even harder. This was a time of extreme emotional, mental suffering.

And so began the shedding of Jesus' holy blood for our sakes. Here in the garden, Jesus shed blood for our emotional and mental disturbances. His own inner turmoil wrought the sacrificial bloodshed for our inner healing. The blood of the Savior was already being poured out for us.

Jesus had been sprawled on the ground, face down, head wrapped within and beneath His prayer shawl. Face down into folded arms, Jesus prayed and wept. His prayer became the prayer of surrender. Tears, sweat, and blood mixed together and stained His prayer cloak and tunic.

As a man, Jesus needed God. As God, He knew all the terror ahead.

He sat up and composed Himself, wiping off the sticky wetness with His prayer cloak. He crawled over to a large olive tree and leaned against it. For some time, He emptied Himself in silent prayer to His Father, present and quiet before Him. Waiting. But the night noises startled Him. His nerves were raw. Like a hunted victim, His senses were acute. Expectant. The angel moved closer to Him and knelt beside Him. Jesus accepted the angel's comfort and leaned on the angel's strength. They were silent together as Jesus filled Himself with resolve. And, the angel prayed . . .

An Angel's Holy Moment

Here, my Lord, rest Your weary head.
Lean on my love and strength.
Now, pray all Your love to Your Father above;
no more words, no more tears, only peace.

From Your Father's side I've come.
And bear no sword nor weapon.
On the strength of Your faith,
With the speed of Your love,
In answer to Your prayer, I've come.

Come, lean upon me as a Son,
O, Most Beloved One.
The war has begun, Prince of Peace!

Relaxed, folded hands;
bended knees, closed eyes.
Quiet mind with sweet release.
So still while eternity waits.

The voice of the Almighty did speak
Through an angel's whisper,
"This is the prayer of surrender, My Son.
Drink from its comfort like wine.
Pass not the dread cup from your lips, My Son,
drink deeply this choice vintage wine."

All silent. All holy. This moment His glory
Did fill me with awe inspired.
With humbled bowed head
In reverence, He said
"Not My will, but Thine be done."

The angel was aware of its own awesome mission, its ministry to the Son of God. What a thing, to strengthen and encourage the Lord of Hosts, the Lord of Glory, the Most High God, the Almighty! He had taken on flesh, but He was still God. The angel wished His disciples would wake up, knowing that He would have preferred their support and comfort in His anguish. It was an awesome, terrible privilege to be a strength to God. He needed support. Nothing like this had ever happened, nor could it ever again. For those sleeping, it was the most tragic missed opportunity. It was the prayer meeting of the ages, and no one showed up to pray with Jesus.

Prayerlessness and unawareness robs us of so much. "The spirit is willing, but the flesh is weak," Jesus had said. How well Jesus understood that!

Twice, Jesus had already gone over to check in with them, having to wake them each time. Why did another garden experience have to prove such disappointment to the One who sought nothing but companionship and faithfulness? There was One in the garden that night who would remain faithful and obedient, the only One who could. He accepted the terrible reality. The desire of His Father. Though He loathed what was ahead of Him, He would endure because He knew how much depended upon Him. After accepting it, He felt the deep joy surrendered obedience brings, becoming strong and even zealous to give Himself. He was ready to face all His enemies. When Jesus heard noises coming from the Kidron Valley, He stood and walked over and knelt next to Peter. He looked again at His three good friends as they slept. He shook Peter's shoulder. "Why are you sleeping? Get up and pray so you will not fall into temptation." Peter was embarrassed and upset with himself for getting caught sleeping again, but he noticed immediately that Jesus seemed back to His old self. Just then the gate to the garden banged, and Jesus looked up to see Judas walking toward Him.

There was a crowd, including temple guards, standing a short distance behind Judas holding torches and weapons. Jesus stood and faced Judas as he came to Him. Smiling, Judas hesitated a moment. Jesus' heart sank as he watched Judas come forward, pretending friendship.

"Friend," Jesus' voice was even, "do what you came for." Judas now stood in front of Him. This betrayal was, to Jesus, very bitter. Judas then took hold of Jesus and embraced and kissed Him on both cheeks. This was the signal Judas was to give the guards, to single out the man they were to arrest. Still pretending, Judas held Him at arms' length, holding Him at His shoulders, as a close friend would with fond regard. But all Jesus could do was stare back—achingly violated. The kiss of betrayal had stunned Him. In a broken voice, filled with incredulous sorrow and compassion, Jesus asked, "Judas, are you betraying the Son of Man . . . with a kiss?" He could hardly say it. Why a kiss? A kiss isn't meant to wound is it? What kind of tragedy play are we acting out? Oh, Judas! Jesus paused for a moment, looking into cold, nervous eyes, searching for a glimpse of remorse. He found none. He took a deep breath and, with determination, looked away from Judas and steadied His gaze on the waiting mob. Judas released his hold on Him; and shame became his new friend instead.

Jesus walked up to the soldiers and Jewish leaders, who stood in front of the crowd. Alone, He faced them and asked, "Who is it you seek?"

They answered, "Jesus of Nazareth."

"I am He." They all fell back from His power.

Then asking a second time He said, "Who is it you seek?"

They answered again, "Jesus of Nazareth," and they carefully ventured forward.

"I told you, I am."

That's when the order was given and He was seized. His hands were tightly bound with ropes. Under all the eyes of heaven, He was forcefully taken from the garden.

This time an angel was posted but had no sword in hand.

And so it was, that the Bridegroom had walked into the garden as the great I AM, as the Great King and Good Shepherd, and walked out of it God's Lamb—to be slaughtered—for His bride.

A Garden in a Cemetery ~

*T*he garden that surrounded a tomb belonged to a rich man. The tomb held the temple of the Creator, the desecrated body of Jesus. The temple had been violently destroyed, forcing the Lord's presence out.

All of heaven witnessed the horror. Myriads of angels could have stormed the forces of evil to easily rescue their Lord. He wouldn't let them. The heavenly witnesses watched in silent awe as the all powerful Lord of Life, who could, at any moment He desired, blow the whole universe away, suffer horrible agony and die.

He used His almighty power to succumb.

Heaven's hosts marveled at the strength of Love. And, they marveled at the weakness of Almighty God—God in so much pain. His majesty, glorious Lord, Most Holy One, Most High—hanging on a cross? Naked and in shame. What a wonder! All for love. The love that took all blame. Heaven turned away no longer wanting to stay. They couldn't look anymore.

When Jesus went death's way, He didn't stay. Instead, He simply passed through. He went there to let His people go. Like Moses, He brought them to the "Promised Land." Now, that was on the Day of the Passover.

A couple of days later, several angels were sent to a garden. They had a pleasant mission. They had messages to give. They were so glad the atrocity was over. The angels were so proud of Jesus, their Soveriegn Lord. The angels saw the women coming. It was just barely light, at dawn. Three women came to the garden and tomb. They were members of the Lord's bride. They had come to care for His body. The angels were filled with sheer joy, so thrilled to tell them the good news. The angels proclaimed, "The Lord is not here, but is risen." They reminded the women that Jesus predicted that He would be delivered into the hands of sinful men, be crucified, and on the third day be raised again. They told the women to go and tell His grieving disciples that He was alive and that He would meet them soon.

But one of the women returned to the tomb. It was Mary Magdalene. She was upset. She had hurried and told the disciples what the angels said. Peter and John returned with her to see for themselves. They saw no angels, but they did see the empty tomb. And they saw the shroud that had been wrapped around their beloved master. They were still too consumed with grief, confusion, and fear to fully understand. They left, bewildered. But Mary didn't leave the garden. How could she? Her Lord was not there. She couldn't understand what the angels had meant. She was distraught. All she could think about was Jesus. Where is He? Who has taken His body, and where? She couldn't be comforted. She loved Him so much.

Since the time she first met Him, she followed Him everywhere He'd let her. He'd freed her from evil spirits. She was *herself* because of Him. And now, still, she was wholly His. How could life go on without Him?

She had stayed in the company of His disciples, traveling on foot all over the country. She had gotten used to camping, cooking meals for large groups, washing and mending clothes. She helped care for the souls that were drawn to Him. She was one of a group of women who traveled and ministered with Jesus and the disciples. It was like some wonderful spell He'd cast on her—she couldn't help but follow Him. He was everything to her. And now He was gone.

She threw herself onto the ground and wept. She had seen it all. How could this have happened? She wished to wake from this tragic nightmare. She didn't care that she had publicly associated herself with Him by standing below His cross. Maybe they'd kill her too. She loved Him more than her own life. She could think of nothing else but Him. When He was on the cross she had to be there too.

Jesus had hung there naked and bleeding. Why this horrific shame? He personified purity. Was He ashamed of His nakedness? Would He rather she didn't see Him this way? But she had not been able to stay away from that cross. Why was He willing to let them do this to Him? She knew of His power.

The Jewish leaders had stood near the cross smugly staring, ridiculing Him. How could they do this to anyone—to one of their own people? He scared them, that's why. He was better than all of them put together. They didn't want the Messiah to come. Why couldn't they accept Him? Why didn't they believe in Him? Anger and hate had begun to consume her as she stood at the cross. Just then, in the midst of her questions and hate, Jesus spoke, even though it pained Him greatly to do so. It was what He said that struck her, as though even now He'd been reading all her thoughts.

He forgave them all. First, His eyes lit upon the soldiers, then moved to the religious ones, then the crowd. He was not only forgiving them: He was asking that His Father would forgive them too. How *could* He?—hanging near death, in sheer agony, humiliated beyond all limits?

"They know not what they do."

Jesus, what are they doing? Who are You? Even the Roman centurion stood in disbelief, glancing at Mary to see if she'd heard what he thought he'd heard. Mary could only answer his questioning eyes by weeping. She wept away her own hatred. And, she wept because there was nothing else she could do.

Throughout the long hours Mary watched and cried. Jesus suffered insults, spitting, cruel joking, and name calling; yet, He never retaliated. He valiantly absorbed the cruelty. She watched Him hang in agony as the hours unmercifully crawled on. She watched His labor to breathe as He wrenched Himself up, standing on His nailed feet, which, because of the angle, also tore into the flesh of His feet. But it was the only way to get air into His lungs. Shooting pain and weakness kept Him from raising Himself often enough. He was suffocating. How long could this go on?

She stared, mesmerized at His hands nailed to the rough, bloodied beam. The nails went through the center hollow spot in His wrists; the bones and flesh of His hands above each nail painfully bore the weight of His body. Those wonderful hands that had reached and touched all who came to Him, healing thousands! How gentle was His loving touch. How often He'd squeeze her hand, or pat her head to show His love or appreciation. She remembered how He would talk using His hands in gestures. His hands—now nailed to a cross with drying deep red streams of blood trickling down His arms. What madness is this?

Her eyes finally had moved to study His face. Was this possible? Was this the gentle, pure face of Rabboni, her teacher? Swollen cheeks, black eyes, even part of His beard had been ripped away. Bloodied and dirty. Face full of pain. Eyes of compassion. Even now, she saw compassion on His face as Jesus loved His mother from the cross, sorry for her pain.

He struggled to speak to John when he appeared at the foot of the cross. John, too, had come close without fear. He loved Jesus with no regard for his own life. Jesus had totally won over John's heart, as He had Mary's. She could tell that Jesus was glad John was there, the only one of the twelve that witnessed Jesus' suffering and death. Jesus spoke with His eyes for a long time, looking from John to His mother and back. Finally, lifting Himself up against the nails longer than usual in order to speak, His endearing words sent her into another bout of weeping. Making a "living will", He introduced them to one another. "Behold, John, your mother. Mother, behold, your son." Obeying his master immediately, John led Jesus' mother away.

Whenever Jesus looked at Mary, she tried hard not to wail, she could hardly bear it. Jesus met her eyes with His and motioned with His head, that she should leave, too. She couldn't leave, though. She stopped crying and held His eyes with hers—those sacred eyes of His—so strikingly filled with love mixed with pain. He wanted her to leave for her own sake, but she just couldn't. She shook her head "No" while covering her mouth with her hands. Jesus closed His eyes. She moved to stand with some other women a short distance away from the cross where she remained until the end.

The hours dragged on. Time became His greatest enemy. He was in tortured agony, hanging in searing pain—enduring, enduring, enduring. His contorted body violently twitched and jerked in spasms. He struggled to stand up less and less on the little ledge of wood that held fast His feet; it wasn't because of the sheering pain from the spike running through the flesh of His feet, it was because He was drained of energy. He was slowly suffocating, unable to breathe while His own weight pressed down upon Him.

She wondered what He was thinking. Sometimes His eyes were open, but most of the time they were squeezed shut. The sun had stopped shining. It grew unusually dark. The shouting and mocking had died away, not from pity, but from fear. The eerie darkness was frightening people away. Most of the crowd dispersed and the afternoon dragged on.

Such was the Savior's agony. Suffocation and heart failure ushered Jesus into death—death for the One who breathes life and love into every living soul. He had hung suspended between heaven and earth on a cross. His cross of agony became a bridge, a crossing-over from death and hell to life and heaven.

Near the bitter end, He rallied. Pushing up against the spikes impaled in His feet, Jesus raised His face and voice to the dark heavens and cried out to His Father. "Eli, Eli, Lama Sebachthani?" He spoke in Hebrew, not Aramaic, from a Scripture—one of the Psalms. It meant: "My God, My God, why have You forsaken Me?" When Mary heard this it frightened her. Never had she seen Him like this. He was shouting in desperation. Mary and those near the cross saw the most pitiful sight ever witnessed. Eternity stood still in time and in judgment. No one really understood what was happening.

After some time, she moved back to stand near the cross. She could see His desperate thoughts were gone. She saw on His face a deep sense of acceptance, or was it accomplishment and satisfaction? It certainly was peace. It was over. She knew He was about to leave. He stood up one last time against the nails. He stood tall, pulled air into His lungs, and shouted, "It is finished!" Then, with His wounded face uplifted and full of holy beauty—which so gripped Mary's soul—He prayed aloud: "Abba! Into Your hands I commit My spirit!" At that moment, though she didn't fully understand why, she never loved her Lord Jesus more.

As Jesus left His body, it fell hard against the stake, the holy head fell limp, the crown of thorns came loose and fell to the ground, and there was a terrible earthquake and a clap of thunder at that moment. The shaking earth ripped the massive, many layered, curtained veil from top to bottom in the holy temple. Never before had the entrance to the Holy of Holies been open until that moment.

Storm clouds unleashed a sudden downpour with lightening and thunder crashes. Everyone at the cross was frightened. Some ran away striking their breasts, afraid of the living God.

It almost seemed like all really was finished, as this holy man had declared. Panic gripped the hearts of almost everyone there, except for the ones weeping and the Roman centurion. He was on his knees, proclaiming that the man he'd just killed was who He had claimed to be. Some were praying. John had returned and was weeping even harder than was Mary. She'd gone over to him and the two stood clinging to each other as the ground tremored beneath them. When John stopped weeping he'd gone into a kind of trance when his eyes rested some time on a little puddle of blood that had formed in a crevice of the rocky ground around the stake. He was remembering the cup of wine Jesus had shared with them at supper the night before. "This cup is the new covenant in My blood, which is poured out for you," Jesus had said. As he stood staring for some time, the rain water carried the red puddle downstream and into the mud and rocky soil of the hillside.

Mary could only look upon her beloved Lord, now dead on the cross, and cry. The earth had opened up wide and almost swallowed her. The physical disturbances around her were nothing in comparison to the emotional ones going on inside of her. She stood by helplessly as His dead body hung there. One of the soldiers, carrying the large hammer, looked up at Him. The soldier had just broken the other criminals' legs to hurry death for them. The soldiers wanted to leave. Fear and ominous feelings gripped everyone. Soon it would be the Sabbath, and the Jews needed this over before then—in order not to disobey their Law. Since Jesus appeared dead, the soldier didn't break His legs, but to make sure He was really dead, he picked up a long spear and thrust it into Jesus' side. Mary and John watched both blood and water pour out. This wound in His side was a great witness of truth. Jesus was surely dead.

Not so obvious at the time was the even greater witness of truth regarding the mysterious. Jesus' side was opened like Adam's to form His Bride—taken from His side—from His own blood and water. This was a physical sign of a spiritual reality: the blood necessary for redemption and the water necessary for spiritual life. Both of these, from His very Life, flowed freely from the broken heart of the Son of God. Another witness of truth: the bones of the Lamb of God were not broken, as was forbidden for the ritual Passover lambs. This, too, had been prophesied about Him in the Psalms. Jesus lingered in extreme agony up until they would have broken His legs. In this way was His longsuffering love proven. He gave as much as He could.

Mary Magdalene stayed while Jesus' body was taken down and wrapped in a shroud with spices. John helped a couple of others carry His body to a garden tomb nearby. It was down and around the same blood-soaked hill. Mary followed and waited to see where He was laid and left after dark with the others.

Sleep was impossible and that Sabbath Day ran together with the next day. She was caught awake in a nightmare.

Jesus was so good. Why did they do this to Him? There in the garden, she cried outloud, "Where have they taken Him?!" She could not be comforted, not at all. She sobbed, pounding the ground.

Jesus had been standing there near her for some time, watching her, knowing all her thoughts. He allowed her pain to cry its way out of her heart for awhile. Then she stood up and approached the burial cave to, again, look for Him. He stepped quietly up behind her. He wanted her to see Him. He was overwhelmed with compassion and love for her. There would be no more waiting for her. She thought He was the gardener. Full of secret delight, knowing she was unaware of His identity, He gently asked, "Why are you crying?" He was bursting to say, "Mary, here I am! Mary, it's Me." He was so thrilled to relieve her distress. He was savoring the gladness of the moment, the sheer joy of it. Then, tenderly, He said her name. "Mary."

No one said her name like He did. His familiar voice . . . In that instant of glorious recognition, she shouted, "Rabboni!" And she threw herself at His feet and clung to Him as if she would never let Him go.

Once again, a garden was a place of delight!

But Jesus needed to go. She must not cling to Him. He needed to go to the Father. The time had come to cling to Him in another way—an even better way.

He went to heaven and sent His Spirit to His beloved until His return. While we wait, we, His bride, are being formed from Him, being made like Him, and coming to know and really love Him. Now Jesus walks with His beloved in another kind of garden. The garden of the bride is a spiritual, mystical garden— true Eden.

A Garden of Spiritual Delight ~

Come, *cling* to Jesus in this new and living way! The following Scriptures and reflections are provided as a means to meet Jesus in this spiritual garden—the "Garden of Eden" restored. You are invited to once again eat from the tree of life. No longer is an angel posted outside its gates to keep us away. God now invites us to partake in His eternal life. Lift up your gates, ye everlasting doors, and let the Lord of glory come in! This inner sanctuary is within your heart, and Jesus has unlocked its gate forever.

> "I have come into my garden, my sister, my bride;
> I have gathered my myrrh along with my spice.
> I have eaten my honeycomb and my honey.
> I have drunk my wine with my milk.
> Eat, O friends;
> Drink and imbibe deeply, O beloved ones."

Song of Songs 5:1

> "Who, after all, is meant by these friends and beloved? The Lord was so enjoying His loved one as a fragrant garden in His own right as her Savior and Lord. It would appear, therefore, that these friends and beloved would indicate that the Three Persons—the whole Trinity—One God—are here together in the receiving of, and in the enjoyment of, all the good of this garden of spiritual fruit now matured in this loved one. It is God alone, and not man, who receives the fruit of a believer's life."

(Watchman Nee writes in Song of Songs, published by Christian Literature Crusade. Used with Permission.)

The bride of Christ is in relationship with Mystery—the Trinity. We have been invited into this love affair that goes on within the Godhead. And, God wants us to drink deeply of this intoxicating drink. This is the greatest joy and it is all mystery and grace!

> "A garden locked is my sister, my bride,
> a rock garden locked, a spring sealed up.
> Your shoots are an orchard of pomegranates
> With choice fruits, henna with nard plants,
> Nard and saffron, calamus and cinnamon,
> With all the trees of frankincense,
> Myrrh and aloes, along with all the finest spices.
> You are a garden spring,
> A well of fresh water,
> And streams flowing from Lebanon."

Song of Songs 4:12

This private garden is where Jesus comes and drinks of the wine of love and joy, and tastes its sweetness like honey. It is where He picks and eats the fruits of her love. There, within her, is the well of living water flowing from His Spirit of Love. Likewise, she has become as a spring of fresh water.

It is so wonderful to think that we can affect His heart and bring Him joy. The soul of His bride says,

> "My lover has gone down to His garden, to the beds of spices to browse in the gardens and to gather lilies. I am my lover's and my lover is mine; He browses among the lilies."

Song of Songs 6:2-3

Prayer, worship, and loving devotion are ways to experience being in the company of the Bridegroom while He abides in this Garden of Delight. It is an inner experience. The intimately divine love relationship in this garden is for God and His bride alone.

"Listen! My lover!
Look! Here he comes,
Leaping across the mountains,
Bounding over the hills.
My lover is like a gazelle or a young stag.
Look! There he stands behind our wall,
Gazing through the windows,
Peering through the lattice.
My lover spoke and said to me,
'Arise, my darling, my beautiful one, and come
with me."

Song of Songs 2:8-10

Standing outside a window and peering in through lattice
means that that person standing against the lattice can easily
see in, but more than likely, is hidden from view from the one(s)
inside. When Jesus sees us, He sees us clearly. He looks very
intently into the "windows" of our houses, our lives, our minds
and hearts. However, we have to be aware that He is there. We
must come close to the lattice, and *earnestly* look for Him if we
want to see Him.

"My lover spoke and said to me,
'Arise, my darling, my beautiful one, and come
with me.
See! The winter is past;
The rains are over and gone.
Flowers appear on the earth;
The season of singing has come,
The cooing of doves is heard in our land.
The fig tree forms its early fruit;
The blossoming vines spread their fragrance.
Arise, come, my darling; my beautiful one,
come with me.'"

Song of Songs 2:10-13

"Behold, you are fair, my love!
Behold, you are fair!
You have dove's eyes behind your veil."

Song of Songs 4:1a

You and I, individually, are this fair, beloved one. Why does our Lord see His maiden as lovely? It is because of the cross. This event happened in the past, but it is also in the constant present. We are being saved every day by His cross of love. Each of us stand at the foot of it, side by side with Jesus' murderers. Our sins hammered those nails into His hands and feet as surely as did His executioners. We can't blame the Sanhedrin or the Romans. Our sins hung Jesus on the cross as surely as they did. Jesus wanted to save His bride. The Pharisees who sent Him to the cross were no different than any of us. Like them, we have misjudged His plans and purposes many times.

Why in the world does He see His bride as beautiful?

It is a mystery. He says that He sees His own righteousness in "her." He sees only her devotion as she stands at the foot of His cross. It has brought her to love Him. And, now, He wants her to come with Him. He draws us to come after Him—to go away with Him.

What does it mean that the voice of the turtledove has been heard in our land? Have you thought about Him as a Dove? (Sometimes we don't see the trees for the forest.) He says to His beloved: "You have dove's eyes."

A dove is quiet, gentle, peaceful, and will look you directly in the eye with singular vision. Singular vision means "eyes for only one thing at a time." "Blessed are the pure in heart for they shall see God." Pure of heart means pure devotion to God with God-centered, singular vision. God-centeredness is purity of heart. Purity means clean and pure. Cleansed and holy. Pruning of the vines ("You are the vine, I am the Branch") brings that purity. Our devotion should bring us to holiness and purity of heart.

He calls His beloved a turtledove throughout the Song. He is calling His mate. Have you ever watched a pair of doves together? They cuddle. Of course, for us to "cuddle" with God means we have to "cling" to Him. He wants us to be in a love relationship with Him. Grace is the only way that can happen. And, we will not stay cuddling all the time. He will lead us from the romantic times of spring to the cleft in the rock, which is in a very steep place. It is a good climb up with Him. It is not on a path well traveled. It involves faith, trust, perseverance, obedience, and hiding in Him—in the cleft of the Rock. In His presence.

The Lord would say to you, precious one,

"O my dove, in the clefts of the rock,
in the secret places of the cliff,
(similar to Moses in the cleft of the rock awaiting to see God)
Let me see your face,
let me hear your voice;
For your voice is sweet,
And your face is lovely."

Song of Songs 2:14

When the Bride first begins to love God for Himself, and not for what He gives to bless and do; but, rather, when the Bride desires God for Himself alone, there is a new flame ignited for her King . . .

"Let him kiss me with the kisses of his mouth—
For your love is better than wine.
Because of the fragrance of your good ointments;
Your name is ointment poured forth;
Therefore the virgins love you.
Draw me away!
We will run after you.

The King has brought me into his chambers."

Song of Songs 1:1-3

Union's Kiss

Bridegroom:
Come within, I bid you, come.
Inside this secret chamber deep
In the place of your own heart
Is where we two should meet

Remove your veil
There's no more need
And let Me see your face
In this secret, holy place

Bride:
My Lord, I dare not
for I have sinned
Ashamed and full of need I am
Your cross has just begun its work
Not yet complete in me

Bridegroom:
We have made for you
garments, rich
A wedding gown, white
and trimmed with gold
Fine silver chains,
adorned with precious jewels
All these we've given you
My lovely bride, to wear

Bride:
Lord, I am not worthy
But your eyes with kindness shine
And all the dark and lonely aches
Depart as love imparts
Shekhinah in my heart

Your costly blood-grown wine
Rich and vibrant in my mouth
It goes down smooth and lifts
my soul now blessed,
higher than before,
filled with life

Across the timeless fathoms deep
His Majesty has reached, and bent
so low to kiss the one He loves
And spent Himself to make us one

With bliss, You fill my soul
Your kiss is so much more
Than can be told
And sweet Your breath, so near
Life's deepest joy to know

Prayer Journal Exercises

1. Using Psalm 45, meditate on our Bridegroom King. Using
    your prayer journal, allow the rich images of these verses
    to enter into your heart. Be careful to listen to the Divine
    whispers or thoughts that God may give as you internalize
    these thoughts.

    "My heart is overflowing with a good theme: I recite my
    composition concerning the King; my tongue is the pen of a
    ready writer. (v. 1)

    "You are fairer than the sons of men; grace is poured
    upon Your lips; therefore God has blessed You forever."
    (v. 2)

    "Your throne, O God, is forever and ever; a scepter of
    righteousness is the scepter of Your kingdom." (v. 6)

    "All Your garments are scented with myrrh and aloes
    and cassia. Out of the ivory palaces, by which they have
    made You glad." (v. 8)

    "Listen, O daughter, consider and incline your ear,
    (v. 10a)

    "So the King will greatly desire your beauty; because
    He is your Lord, worship Him." (v. 11)

    "The royal daughter is all glorious within the palace;
    her clothing is woven with gold." (v. 13)

2. Here is a meditation for "Blessed are the pure in heart, for
    they shall see God." If God said: "Ask Me for anything and
    I will give it to you. Anything at all. However, there is one
    stipulation. I will give you anything you ask for, but in
    exchange you will never be able to see My face." Could
    anything be worth it? Can you imagine never being able to
    see His face? No? Then you have a pure heart—and you

will see God. Isn't it amazing how great the little mustard seed of faith is (God's great gift of grace) that is firmly planted within our hearts? Isn't seeing Jesus' face worth dying for? Isn't seeing Jesus what you *really* want the most? Pray and *realize* that—let it sink in. Then, write your thoughts and feelings about this in your journal.

4. If the weather is good or your circumstances permit, go for a walk with Jesus. Keep your mind on Him the whole time. Listen. Look. Be open to whatever dialogue may come. Look for Him in nature and in all that surrounds the two of you while you walk. Examine a leaf or flower, a frozen puddle, a bare tree or whatever the season brings you. Watch bees, ants, clouds, or whatever captures your attention. Listen to the outdoor noises: birds singing, wind; listen to the silent things: stars, sunrise, crops growing. Enjoy God's creation with Him. See if God doesn't speak to you through them. Many wonderful lessons can be learned from nature. Perhaps you will enjoy His presence silently. When you return, be sure to record the highlights of your experiences in your journal.

5. Write God a psalm, a poem, or a love song. Can you imagine the kind of New Testament psalm David would write if given the chance? It doesn't have to be long or profound—just real—from your heart. Be yourself. Enjoy being yourself with God. He loves you so much.

Chapter Seven

A CONSUMING FIRE

*F*ierce, raging fire burns in the heart of God. This fire is passionate love.

> "Wake up! Strengthen what remains and is about to die, for I have not found your deeds complete in the sight of my God. Remember, therefore, what you have received and heard; obey it, and repent. But if you do not wake up, I will come like a thief, and you will not know at what time I will come to you. . . . Anyone who overcomes will, like them, be dressed in white. I will never erase his name from the book of life, but will acknowledge his name before my Father and His angels. He who has an ear, let him hear what the Spirit says to the churches." (Rev. 3:2-6)
>
> "You have persevered and have endured hardships for My name, and have not grown weary. Yet I hold this against you: you have forsaken your first love. Remember the height from which you've fallen! Repent and do the things you did at first. If you do not repent, I will come to you and remove your lampstand from its place." (Rev. 2:4-6)
>
> "These are the words of the Amen the Faithful and true witness, the ruler of God's creation. I know your deeds, that you are neither cold nor hot. I wish you were either one or the other! So, because you are lukewarm—neither hot nor cold—I am about to spit you out of My mouth. You say, 'I am rich; I have acquired wealth and

do not need a thing.' But you do not realize that you are wretched, pitiful, poor, blind and naked. I counsel you to buy from Me gold refined in the fire, so you can become rich; and white clothes to wear, so you can cover your shameful nakedness; and salve to put on your eyes, so you can see.

Those whom I love I rebuke and discipline. So be earnest, and repent. Here I am! I stand at the door and knock. If anyone hears My voice and opens the door, I will go in and eat with him, and he with Me.'" (Rev. 3:14b-20)

There is mincing of words, no "nice" speech coming from the Word of God to the seven churches. Our glorious risen Bridegroom is a fireball of passion and zeal. John the Baptist said of Him: "'He will baptize you with the Holy Spirit and with fire. His winnowing fork is in His hand to clear His threshing floor and to gather the wheat into His barn, but He will burn up the chaff with unquenchable fire.' And with many other words John exhorted the people and preached the good news to them." (Luke 3:16-18)

To us John's words are shocking, strong and paradoxical. "He will burn up the chaff in unquenchable fire." Right after that powerful word the paragraph closes saying that this was *good* news!

A picture of Jesus full of bright light, eyes of fire, holding a pitch fork in hand, ready to throw "the chaff" into eternal, unquenchable fire . . . This is *good* news?

Most certainly.

God's love is a consuming fire. He shoots flaming arrows of Love into hearts. These are "flaming arrow" words. He aims at dead hearts— "Awake!" God visits humankind in burning bushes of life events. Some saints have been burned at the stake for such love. God is a fiercely passionate fire of Love. One can't get close to Him without paying the price—God's flame—Love—burns and consumes until all becomes one. This divine love is holy.

Many Christians try to measure up to God's standards of holiness. There are many "letter of the law" Pharisees and shallow believers in our churches today. Many are really lukewarm. Much of Christianity today is "cultural" more than anything else—often little more than religious traditions and codes of conduct to be followed. Jesus' description of Christianity and holiness is this: Love God with your whole being and strength and your neighbor as yourself.

How does one love God entirely? The only way is to be smitten in the heart by God's flaming arrow. The arrow will lodge itself deep in the heart of God's beloved victim. It will burn there over the whole of one's lifetime until the heart eventually becomes that holy flame—one in union with God's passionate, affectionate, life-giving, love.

Jesus is a bridegroom. His hope is to be loved like one. The flame of love is truly a mixture of all loves: phileos, eros, and agape. There are stages and progressions to pass through on our way to union.

Fear of God (discerning knowledge) is the beginning of wisdom. However, passionate love with God is a love relationship. God's call is that of a Lover for the beloved—God and a soul. It can seem terribly inappropriate to think of such intimate familiarity with Jesus, the awesome King of Glory; however, God is the One calling us into this love-union. We can hardly accept this. It seems "too good to be true!" How can our hearts and minds allow us entrance into this experience when God is all holy, and we so unholy? Love and worship will bring us into the Holy of Holies. There we behold God in humility—our only appropriate response to His presence. There we will be God's entirely—one with God. This is a spiritual place.

Spousal love with God is what *He* wants. This experience fulfills the first part of God's command to love Him (because this is why we were created). This love-union with God is as much a mystery as is human marriage (in its purest form), which is really only a shadow of spousal love with God.

Lovemaking is an expression and celebration of a married couple's love. It is called union. To make a point, it helps to reflect on the fact that all natural, created things are but imitations of the original, mere symbols of spiritual reality, like shadows from true light.

Love does not give in order to receive but hopes for return of love, and when it is, great pleasure results. Sexual pleasure is a truly beautiful and sacred gift from God. If it is spoiled, it is due to our sin and selfishness. Miraculously, because of the Creator's genius, lovemaking is a blissful kind of dying and resurrection. By giving oneself to the other, simultaneously resurrection/ecstasy occurs bringing extreme pleasure to both the giver and receiver. Lovemaking is not the love itself, it is a celebration of love. It is love expressed—giving oneself to the other. And, sometimes a new life is conceived (a new, whole individual made from the two). Even if a child is not the fruit of the union, the celebrative act of union brings a stronger bond of unity between the two of them in their love relationship.

In spiritual union between Jesus and His bride there is similar experience. During prayer, in quiet times, in a secluded place, one can enter into solitude which is full of the presence of God. There is an inward awareness of God's Presence. Love is expressed, first in dialogue, or meditation, worship, then in contemplation (inward awareness)—silent, non-communicative, love is exchanged. The soul opens "herself" fully, abandoningly, to her Lover. "She" will give Him anything and everything "she" is. He gives Himself to "her." He expresses His love passionately.

When we exchange love to one another in this kind of prayer, there is an opening of ourselves to Him. In dying we live. In giving we receive.

John Michael Talbot, singer, songwriter and founder of a contemplative order, in his book *The Lover and The Beloved*, describes this spiritual love relationship with God. When describing prayer and spiritual union with God, he writes:

> "It all comes down to love. He touches me with love, and I respond in love. This mystery is beyond my words. I laugh and I cry. I shout in loud praise, and I am reduced to silence. He removes a veil between us and reveals wonders far to my right and far to my left. The King of Glory has entered into my very soul, and my

heart expands to the point of near explosion. I truly believe that were my divine lover to reveal too much of Himself to me at once, my heart would explode and I would die."

In the same book, John Michael Talbot shares what he's learned from Franciscan writings:

"I am reminded of the Franciscan hermit and contemporary of St. Francis (of Assisi), Brother John of Alverna, who is said to have experienced such knowledge during a rapture. One story about him says that while first meditating on the humanity of Christ he was overcome by the Spirit and his soul was drawn out of his body, and his soul and heart were burning a hundred times more than if he had been in a furnace.

Afterward God raised him above every creature so that his soul was absorbed and assumed into the abyss of the Divinity and Light, and it was buried in the ocean of God's Eternity and Infinity, to the point he could not feel anything that was created or formed or finite or conceivable or visible which the human heart could conceive or the tongue could describe.

And he felt the eternal infinite love which led the Son of God to incarnate out of obedience to His Father. And by meditating and pondering and weeping on the path of the Incarnation and the Passion of the Son of God, he came to unutterable insights."

(*The Lover and the Beloved* by John Michael Talbot; The Crossroad Publishing, 1985. Used with permission.)

Our most worthy cause is to burn with divine ferocity and become one with God. Jesus came to earth to set it ablaze. The fires He sets are within hearts. His love can be a ravenous forest fire that consumes everything alive and whole. Those who truly follow Jesus all the way will be as William McNamara says, " . . . totally called, awesomely marked, thoroughly spent, and imperiously sent. . . . The life of any person of outstanding quality is borne forward on the wings of a great passion." (*Mystical Passion: The Art of Christian Loving;* Amity House.)

The greatest passion of all passions is God's love. If one is laid waste by it, that person will achieve purity of heart and will see God—the consummation of our deepest longing.

In 397 A.D. Augustine of Hippo wrote a number of philosophical and theological treatises, including *Confessions* and *On Seeing God.* He was a mature man when he came to faith in Jesus, having spent a wild life as a youth. Augustine was most concerned with God's great commandment: To love God with all of his soul. It began the dialogue with God that he wrote about in *Confessions.* His most famous quote is: "You have made us to be *toward* You, and our heart is restless until it rests in You." He declared that our being made by Him was a call to union with Himself. Augustine's experience of Jesus led him to mystical union with Him. He wrote:

> "Late have I loved you, O Beauty, so ancient and so new, late have I loved You! And behold, You were within me and I was outside, and there I sought for You, and in my deformity I rushed headlong into the well-formed things that You have made. You were with me, and I was not with You. Those outer beauties held me far from You, yet if they had not been in You, they would not have existed at all. You called, and cried out to me and broke open my deafness; You shone forth upon me and You scattered my blindness: You breathed fragrance, and I drew in my breath and I now pant for You: I tasted and I hunger and thirst; You touched me, and I burned for Your peace."

> (*Augustine of Hippo: Selected Writings* - The Classics of Western Spirituality; translated and Introduction by Mary T. Clark; published by Paulist Press. Used with permission.)

Augustine taught that "although we have no power of seeing, there is a grace of meriting that we may be able to see." Desire to see God is the only condition necessary for seeing Him. It is God who gives the desire and God who fulfills it. God is not sought by eyes but by desire, nor is He found except through love. Only by loving do we know love.

Lovers of God live in a paradise (which means "living in happiness"). Augustine said that Paradise is knowledge of God's presence in the universe and in ourselves and is not always received wholly, but according to each one's capacity. He wrote a lot about seeing God. The bottom line was "the pure in heart will see God." There will be a beatific vision—in heaven after our resurrection when we will see Him as He is.

It is His ineffable glory, who He truly is, that we long to see—all His Goodness we are so attracted to. We are like Moses who was seeing God face-to-face but still yearned to see God in reality (in His glory).

Augustine taught that seeing God is perceiving Him when He *seems* absent. The disciples saw Him and "didn't see Him" Philip said: Show us the Father and that will be enough." Jesus responded, "He that sees Me sees the Father also." They were seeing Him but were not "seeing" Him. Yet, we "see" Him when we cannot see Him. Augustine emphasized that the "pure in heart" would see God. Purity speaks of single-hearted devotion—having "eyes" only for God. Then He is seen. Pure devotion, through the darkness of faith, enables sight of the ineffable Light. It is a dazzling darkness.

Prayer is a means of seeing, hearing and experiencing God. Ideally, we would abide in constant, continual prayer (unceasing). All of life can become prayer, if one is in love and continually abides in God. Even when preoccupied with business, or when busyness keeps us from quiet prayer, our hearts can always be *toward* Him through our commitment and faith to live wholly for Jesus. All of life can become union and communion with the Great Lover.

Alan Jones, a modern writer, in his attempt to describe mystical prayer (contemplation) describes it more like a life-style of prayer than a kind of prayer. He writes: "If we are designed to be in communion with God, if God is our Lover, then we have to indulge in the things that lovers do. The lover wishes always to be in the loved one's presence, and to gaze and to hold. The name for this loving regard is contemplation."

Contemplation is mystical experience with God—knowing and being known by the Mystery of all that God is. It can be an acute awareness of God's presence but often there is no felt awareness, and our prayer encounter often involves silence with no sensory perceptions. Yet, this prayer is spiritually full of the fire of God's presence and love. As deep calls to deep, the sensory gives way to the spiritual experience of God. Intimate oneness of being enveloped within the Ineffable occurs and is more aptly described as experiencing God in the "cloud of unknowing.*"

The life from such experience will be a life of love coming from being in union with God. John of the Cross said: "Contemplation is nothing else but a secret, peaceful and loving infusion of God, which, if admitted, will set the soul on fire with the spirit of love." Augustine wrote:

> "My whole heart I lay upon the altar of Thy praise, a whole burnt offering of praise I offer Thee... Let the flame of Thy love set on fire my whole heart, let nought in me be left to myself, nought wherein I may look to myself, but may I wholly burn towards Thee, wholly be on fire towards Thee, wholly love Thee, as though set on fire by Thee."

(Ibid.)

The flaming love of God is both pain and glory—suffering and ecstasy. The call of the Bridegroom begins with the kisses of His mouth. The beloved becomes intimately enamored by all His goodness. However, the bride will eventually climb upon the cross to join her Beloved there. The bride's soul must be purified and must join the sufferings of her Love.

The way of the cross is the way Jesus tells us we must follow. God's love brings everyone to faith-filled surrender. Abandonment to divine providence, fully trusting God in the day to day, everyday events of life causes one to truly live in love-union with God.

When in love, the beauty and goodness of the "other" attracts and compels us to oneness. All of life revolves around the passionate love for the other, driven by desires to be together, to be united, to "give oneself" to the other. That is, precisely, what happens with spousal love-union with God. God's love "takes over" one's life, becoming the reason for existence. It is mutual. He is driven to give Himself, all His love, to His beloved. His love is the highest of all loves and is the most demanding, but the most rewarding. We will never be fulfilled until we are in complete spousal love-union with Him. In *Crucified Love* by Robin Maas, she writes:

> "What usually captures us mentally and emotionally is the quality of attractiveness. Something beautiful beckons us into relationship. It may be physical beauty; it may be beauty of soul. Whatever it is, when it calls to us it is compelling, and because we have been made to love the beautiful, the good, and the true, we want to respond. To respond to that irresistibly attractive and exclusive beckoning, we must let go all other attachments—all those possessions that in actuality possess us—all our personal hopes, dreams, ambitions, and loves; and we must exchange them for Christ's—His hopes, dreams, ambitions, and loves. For that is what union with God is all about—to be so hopelessly in love that nothing will satisfy our desires unless it first satisfies the One we love. . . . Perfect love loves that which deserves no love. And God, the perfect Lover, is crazy in love with all of us."

> (*Crucified Love: The Practice of Christian Perfection* by Robin Maas; Abingdon Press; 1989. Used with permission.)

The invitation into the flaming, spousal love of Jesus is to all His followers. "Would that she would know Me and love Me as I love her!" This intuitive revelation has been given to many by His Holy Spirit. He declares this deeply in hearts who know intimacy with Him. Jesus will return for a Bride, spotless and holy. The Bride of a Jewish Messiah, the entire Church, will come together in unity to love Him as He deserves—with fervor and passion. Together, with our Jewish believing brothers and sisters, we will anxiously await His return. When Christians from all tongues and cultures experience bridal-love corporately, and worship Him in unity, lift up your heads ye everlasting doors and see the King of Glory come in! This will usher Jesus' return to Jerusalem. This is the Bride He is waiting for! When His Bride loves Him like a Bride, we will be His entirely—pure and holy. Then the days of the New Jerusalem will begin.

What the whole world desires today, more than ever before, is to experience the virtue of God's passion. Society's explosive yearnings: its addictions, sexual immoralities, greed, and violence is a cry for passion—God's passionate love and meaningful purpose in life. Life is meant to be a love affair. Life is meant to be lived with vitality, aliveness, joy, creativity, meaning, and zeal. Jesus—His life—is our way. Jesus, the freest, happiest, most passionate man who ever lived, broke through all the trappings, boundaries, and emptiness of death (life apart from God). Jesus is the passionate love of God—fully human, fully divine—He is our bridge, our link, to God's eternal, glorious life—to union with God. Our human adventure is to become true lovers—*like* Jesus—and *with* Jesus—and *in* Jesus.

God will lead us out from the bed chamber to leap across mountains with Him. He will send us into every corner, hovel, house, and castle to love and serve the world. The second half of the great command: "Love your neighbor as yourself," comes filled with the passion of the bedroom but, as His spouse, we will rise from there to tend His household. And even more wonderful, it is the spousal flame of love that will carry us beyond this life, beyond the grave, to the heights of our eternal, glorious consummation with God—and into the glorious days of the New Jerusalem.

God is singing us a passionate love song: "Place Me like a seal over your heart, like a seal over your arm; for love is as strong as death, its jealousy unyielding as the grave. It burns like a blazing fire, like a mighty flame. Many waters cannot quench love, rivers cannot wash it away." (Song of Songs 8:6-7)

This pledge of God has the sense of unmitigated wildness— His love is as strong as death. Who can escape it? His love is as jealous and unyielding as the grave. How can we flee from it? His flaming wildfire of love cannot be quenched by floods nor rivers. The Singer poetically proclaims His immeasurable, unspeakable love. It is something too profound to describe. It had to be sung. One day the Singer showed us His measureless, unspeakable love. On Calvary. There for all to witness was the truest description of love. The extravagant Singer fulfilled His own song. Today, as we remember, He continues to bid us to come into union.

Holy Communion

Come to holy union, come
My body and My blood becomes
One with you, part of you, My love

You say it's all been done by grace
Rightly so, you do not know
This Mystery feeds itself in love

I give Myself to you, dear one
So will you come, unbound
Hold nothing back or from?

And let yourself be part of Me
Yes, this, too, is mystery
The two of us are one

Holy Communion is a holy God encounter, to be celebrated until Jesus returns for His bride. Whenever we receive the sacred elements of the body and blood of our Savior through that redeeming wine and life-sustaining bread, the communicants partake in a kind of love-ritual with Jesus. It is a vivid, living picture, a dramatic enactment, that each time becomes true experience of union with God.

This new love covenant ritual Jesus ordained immediately before His crucifixion was one of mystery and prophetic fulfillment. Little did His twelve disciples know that that holy Passover meal would become the focal point in history, when for the first time, these famous words were accomplished: "God and man at table are sat down." Restored communion. The Old Covenant met the New. Jesus died for us, saved us, and now comes and abides in us. This is the great happening of redemption. God's redeeming power was fulfilled through the shadows of the Passover remembrances when Jesus became every believer's Passover "by the blood of the Lamb." We know that that Last Supper became the First Communion with God— it became the central part of the believing community's spiritual life then and now. It is still an important experience for each of us in our own relationship with Jesus. He told us to receive Him in this manner, in memory of what He has done, until He returns for us—His bride.

Similar to taking vows to love each other, Jesus gives Himself to the one He loves. The one who receives this gift of Holy Communion, the receiving of the sacred elements of Jesus' body and blood, is by no means making less of a commitment in return. Jesus gave Himself through His actions. Holy Communion would have no meaning without the crucifixion. For the sake of His beloved, He loved enough to give His life in order that His beloved would live in union with Him. He left us a mystical ritual that brings everything close, making our experience with Him intimately *real.* It becomes a ceremony that expresses and celebrates, even facilitates, communion with our spiritual Bridegroom. This experience is an expression of love and union.

It is also a lifetime process. As in any spousal relationship, there is a painful stripping away of ourselves so that we are remade to better complement the other. This is not pleasant.

Yet, it does bring true union. It is that way with God. We will be changed, painfully, dying to be reborn, over and over. If this does not occur, then the experience of union is not authentic. The union will come from "first love" heights of commitment and passion. It is our affectionate devotion that will ignite transformation into His image. The more we know God the more we will know ourselves. This love relationship will change us from self-centeredness to God-centeredness and wholeness. Our ego-self will continually die, as we become transformed from the inside out, until our final breath. Paradoxically, as we breathe God's life, our life in God will birth our true selves. You and I will become the wonderful real self that God has been creating since the moment He first "conceived" us. We are developing into His "beloved" so that we might be truly one with Him.

Joann Nesser, Founder and Director of Christos Center for Spiritual Formation in Lino Lakes, MN, says that even our prayer experience is like a journey from self to God:

> "When we are serious about growing deeper in an intimate love relationship with God, it is important to understand that our spiritual life is a journey and that just as we grow, change, and mature in our natural lives, so we grow, change, and mature in our spiritual lives. As these changes take place, our prayer will also change. The kind of prayer that we pray in the early stages of spiritual growth will not be fulfilling to the mature Christian. The soul who is hungry for God, who is longing for deep, fulfilling relationship with God must allow the Holy Spirit freedom to change the way of praying from one stage to the next.
>
> Prayer is a journey, a journey from self to God, from self-centeredness to God-centeredness. God's desire is for us to grow more and more in oneness with God and with each other. The closing prayer of Jesus' life recorded in John 17 asks that we would be one with God, our Creator,

and each other. God is continually reaching out to us, loving us, creating us, drawing us near. God is forever drawing us deeper into loving union. The whole of our Christian life is a response to that loving call. Our response must be one of seeking and responding. God is the initiator, we are the responders. God calls, we answer. God reaches out to us in love, we respond to that love. The beginning of a prayer journey is saying "Yes" to God's transforming love.

God has promised that if we seek we shall find. Scripture says, 'I know the plans I have for you,' says the Lord, 'plans for welfare and not for evil, to give you a future and a hope. Then you shall call upon me and come and pray to me, and I will hear you. You will seek me and find me; when you seek me with all your heart, I will be found by you.'"

(Prayer: Journey from Self to God by Joann Nesser. Christos Center for Spiritual Formation, 1212 Holly Drive, Lino Lake, MN 55038. Used with Permission.)

This is a call to spousal love-union. More and more people are awakening to the call of the Bridegroom. Union with the Bridegroom not only is a growing process for each of us individually, it is also for the corporate Bride. The entire Church is progressing into union with God. Jesus prayed for it. This union will make us all one with each other in Him. It will not come by way of compromise or doctrinal change. The Bride must first come to love and appreciate each other's differences. This will come most easily because of the passionate flaming love of our Spouse! Many are awakening to the call of the Dove— to let the Spirit do whatever God wants in us. God is pouring out Pentecost flames of fire upon people and churches today. God's anointing and outpouring (God's presence) is taking many forms (not necessarily what would "fit" terminologies either). Charismatic/Pentecostal fervor is not all that is being described here. It is only a part of the many expressions of it. God is much bigger than experiences found in various groups or movements. God is bigger than all our various faith traditions. God is in relationships with persons, churches, and ministries. God does, through His people, whatever He wants whenever He wants (if people are open to His love and Spirit). Worship varies all over the world. How God longs to bring us all together in loving unity of heart and spirit. His Holy Spirit is working to accomplish this. Catholics, Evangelicals, Charismatics, Eastern Orthodox, Messianic Jews, mainline Protestants, denominations, non-denominations, Contemplatives, some are quiet, some are loud, some dance, some don't—common is: our hope, faith, and love for Jesus—and from that, love and unity with each other.

God enjoys the diversity in all of us as much as He delights in both daisies, roses, and cactus. Would the God who created penguins, lions, star fish and peacocks (they praise God by their sheer existence) create less variety in His people and churches (who were made to love and know Him)? Some of us dance with joy and lift His heart, some are rapt in ecstasies of prayer-fervent love that reaches His nostrils like smoke and incense. Which does *He* prefer? Some find Him through intensive study, pulling out the Lexicons from library shelves; some find Him sitting with monks during echoing choruses of chanting the Psalms during Liturgy of the Hours. Does God love the sound of the long blast of the ram's horn during Messianic worship, as hearts are swept up in adoration, and believers fall to their knees? Does He prefer melodies of harp as a gathering of Contemplatives bask in His presence after long periods of silence? God delights in all! "Come, My beloved, let us go forth . . . There I will give you My love . . . All manner, new and old, which I have laid up for you, My beloved." (Song of Songs 7)

Oh, that we might all grasp what Jesus so diligently prayed for. It was so much on His mind as He faced the cross:

> "I do not pray for these alone, but also for those who will believe in Me through their word; that they all may be one, as You, Father, are in Me, and I in You; that they also may be one in us, that the world may believe that You sent Me." (John 17:20-21)

May we all enter into this mystery of spousal union with The Blessed Trinity. It is a lofty, heady truth—that we can love God and be loved by Him in spousal love-union. The beginning of such experience is to simply accept it. This experience of bridal mysticism has a long history. It was first revealed to Israel by Yahweh. Christian spirituality today is discovering that this call of the Divine Spouse is what will most likely unite the Church into one (in answer to Jesus' last priestly prayer). The consuming fire of God—passionate love—will melt away our divisions, barriers, and walls. True unity will come when we celebrate the love of God through diversity. May we come to embrace the beauty and goodness of our uniquenesses and individualities within the Mystical Temple—His Bride.

"I am My beloved's and His desire is toward me." The call of the Bridegroom is the call to love!—passionate and consuming love. We are experiencing the outpouring of God's love and Spirit in our days.

There is one holy communion of saints. We can also unite our hearts with those who have gone on before us. We have a rich inheritance from others who have been set aflame by God's passion and love. Their writings; stories of their lives; poetry, paintings, and art have been left to us. Simply sitting in an older church, in almost any city or country in the world, one can look and see Jesus pictured in the colorful stained glass windows. All throughout Christian history, lovers of our Lord have attempted to share about love and union with Him through art. Sometimes God's love is best expressed through the eyes of a poet, an artist, or a mystic—a person who embraces Mystery and then tries to show it. It is like coming into the Holy of Holies, and being touched by the very Presence of God there within the centermost part of our beings. Such spiritual experience is hard to describe. It is like trying to describe a beautiful, colorful, sunset to a person born blind. But, all throughout Christian history, lovers of Jesus have attempted to share about love and union with God through the use of poetry and spiritual literature. Perception of God and the exchange of love with Him comes only through personal faith and experience. The artists can only point the way. We must "open" our eyes and look, and God must turn on the "Light" so that we can see. Similar to stained glass windows, when the

"Sonlight," the Holy Spirit, shines through these symbolic images, sometimes we can get a glimpse of God's face—Love's face.

The following are ancient poems and prayers to act as a kind of stained glass window. (Credit is given when possible.)

I ask You, Lord Jesus,

to develop in me, your lover,
an immeasurable urge towards you,
an affection that is unbounded,
a longing that is unrestrained,
a fervour that throws caution to the winds!
The more worthwhile our love for you,
all the more pressing does it become.
Reason cannot hold it in check,
fear does not make it tremble,
wise judgment does not temper it."

Richard Rolle
(14th Century, England)

O honeyed flame, sweeter than all sweet,

delightful beyond all creation!
My God, my Love, surge over me, pierce me by your love,
wound me with your beauty.
Surge over me, I say, who am longing for your comfort.
Reveal your healing medicine to your poor lover.
See, my one desire is for you; it is you my heart is seeking.
My soul pants for you; my whole being is athirst for you.
Yet you will not show yourself to me; you look away;
you bar the door, shun me, pass me over;
You even laugh at my innocent sufferings.
And yet you snatch your lovers away from all earthly things.
You lift them above every desire for worldly matters.
You make them capable of loving you—
and love you they do indeed.
So they offer you their praise in spiritual song
which bursts out from that inner fire;
they know in truth the sweetness of the dart of love.
Ah, eternal and most lovable of all joys,
you raise us from the very depths,
and entrance us with the sight of divine majesty so often!
Come into me, Beloved!
All ever I had I have given up for you;
I have spurned all that was to be mine,
That you might make your home in my heart,
and I your comfort.
Do not forsake me now, smitten with such great longing,
whose consuming desire is to be amongst those who love you.
Grant me to love you,
to rest in you,
that in your kingdom I may be worthy
to appear before you world without end.

Richard Rolle

(Both of Richard Rolle's poems are taken from *The
Fire of Love,* Translated into modern English with
an introduction by Clifton Wolters, Penguin Books.)

*A*ll deeds are accomplished in passion.

If the fiery love of God grows cold in the soul,
the soul dies.
And, in a certain sense, God dies also.

The divine countenance
is capable of maddening and driving
all souls out of their senses
with longing for it.
When it does this by its very divine nature
it is thereby drawing all things to itself.
Every creature —whether it knows it or not—seeks repose.

Do you want to know what goes on in the core of the Trinity?
I will tell you.
The Father laughs and gives birth to the Son.
The Son laughs back at the Father and gives birth to the
Spirit.
The whole Trinity laughs and gives birth to us.

All things love God.

The path of which I have spoken is beautiful and pleasant
and joyful and familiar. Let whoever has found this way, seek
no other and you shall find that God who is whole and entire
will possess you whole and entire.

Meister Eckhart, 13th Century, Germany
Source of quote unknown.

Aspirations of the Soul After Christ

(Madame Jeanne Guyon, 16th Century, France)

My Spouse!

In whose presence I live,
Sole object of all my desires,
Who knowest what a flame I conceive,
And canst easily double its fires;
How pleasant is all that I meet!
From fear of adversity free,
I find even sorrow made sweet,
Because 'Tis assigned me by Thee.

Transported I see Thee display
Thy riches and glory divine;
I have only my life to repay,
Take what I would gladly resign.
Thy will is the treasure I seek,
For Thou art as faithful as strong;
There let me, obedient and meek,
Repose myself all the day long.

My spirit and faculties fail;
Oh finish what Love has begun!
Destroy what is sinful and frail,
And dwell in the soul Thou has won!
Dear theme of my wonder and praise,
I cry, who is worthy as Thou!
I can only be silent and gaze;
'Tis all that is left to me now.
Oh glory, in which I am lost,
Too deep for the plummet of thought!
On an ocean of Deity toss'd
I am swallow'd, I sink into nought.
Yet lost and absorb'd as I seem,
I chant to the praise of my King;
And though overwhelm'd by the theme,
Am happy whenever I sing.

Divine Love

(Author known as "T.P.")

*I*n the Paradise of glory

Is the Man Divine;
There my heart, O God, is
tasting
Fellowship with Thine.
Called to share
Thy joy unmeasured,
Now is heaven begun;
I rejoice with Thee, O Father,
In Thy glorious Son.

Where the heart of God is
resting,
I have found my rest;
Christ who found me in the
desert,
Laid me on His breast.
There in deep unhindered
fullness
Doth my joy flow free—
On through everlasting ages,
Lord, beholding Thee.

Round me is creation
groaning,
Death, and sin, and care;
But there is a rest remaining,
And my Lord is there.

There I find a blessed stillness
In His courts of love;
All below but strife and
darkness,
Cloudless peace above.

'Tis a solitary pathway
To that fair retreat—
Where in deep and sweet
communion
Sit I at His feet.
In that glorious isolation,
Loneliness how blest,
From the windy storm and
tempest
Have I found my rest

Learning from Thy lips
forever
All the Father's heart,
Thou hast, in that joy
eternal,
Chosen me my part.
There, where Jesus, Jesus
only,
Fills each heart and tongue,
Where Himself is all the
radiance
And Himself the song.

Canticle II of The Canticle of the Sun   (Francis of Assisi, 12th Century, Italy)

Love sets me all on fire,

Love sets me all on fire.

Into Love's fire I'm cast
By my sweet Bridegroom
new,
As on the ring he passed,
This loving Lamb me threw
Into a prison fast.
He pierced me through and
through,
And broke my heart at last.
Love sets me all on fire.

He pierced my heart, and, lo!
On earth my body lay;
The shaft from Love's
crossbow
Hath rent my heart away.
He aimed a mighty blow,
Then peace to war gave way;
I die of sweetest woe.
Love sets me all on fire.

I die of sweetest woe,
No wonder, for the aim
That struck me such a blow,
From Love's own lances
came,
A hundred arms' length—
know,
The blade that pierced my
frame,
And laid my body low.
Love sets me all on fire.

He aimed his blows so fast,
I thrilled with agony;
I took a shield at last;
'Twas no avail to me,
His darts anew he cast,
And struck so mightily,
That all my strength was past.
Love sets me all on fire.

So hard his blows that I
Found all resistance vain;
Knowing that I must die,
I cried: "Oh, spare my pain!"
But hopeless was my cry,
For he began again,
A new device to try.
Love sets me all on fire.

And now he cast at me
So heavy stones and great,
Each one of them would be
A thousand pounds in weight.
'Twas vain to count them, he
Took aim so sure and straight,
And hurled so rapidly.
Love sets me all on fire.

He aimed his darts so well,
None ever glanced astray,
Prone on the ground I fell,
All helpless there I lay,
Spent and immovable.
Whether I'd passed away,
Or lived, I could not tell.
Love sets me all on fire.

But, lo! I did not die.
For my beloved Lord,
To crown his victory,
My life anew restored,
So keen and fresh, and I
That moment could have soared
To join the saints on high.
Love sets me all on fire.

In life and limb restored,
And full of courage new,
Again I drew my sword,
And to the battle flew;
Once more with him I warred,
And when I fought anew,
I conquered Christ my Lord.
Love sets me all on fire.

When Christ I overthrew,
Again was peace restored,
For well I knew how true
The love of Christ my Lord.
And now, an ardor new
Within my heart is poured.
I burn with love anew
For Christ my Spouse adored.
Love sets me all on fire,
Love sets me all on fire.

(Taken from *St. Francis of Assisi: The Best from All His
Works;* The Christian Classics Collection; Abridged and
edited by Stephen Rost, Thomas Nelson Publishers, c1989.
Used with permission.)

The Living Flame of Love

*(John of the Cross,
16th Century, Spain)*

 Living flame of love

how tenderly you wound
the deepest center of my soul!
Since now no more you afflict me,
bring all, if you will, to a happy ending;
break the web of this sweet encounter.

O sweet cautery!
O delectable wound!
O gentle hand! O delicate touch!
that tastes of eternal life,
and pays every debt!
In killing you have changed death to life

O lamps of fire!
in whose splendors
the deep caverns of feeling,
which were once obscure and blind,
with exquisite loveliness
give forth both warmth and light to their Beloved!

How gently and lovingly
you awaken in my breast
where secretly, alone, you dwell;
and in your sweet breathing
filled with good and glory
how delicately you make me fall in love!

(Taken from *The Living Flame of Love: Saint John of the
Cross; Simplified Version with Notes*, John Vernard, OCD;
E.J. Dwyer; c1990.)

The Spiritual Canticle

John of the Cross (1586 A.D.)

Prologue:

1.

*I*t would be foolish to think

that expressions of love
arising from mystical understanding
are fully explainable.
However, "the Spirit of the Lord aids our weakness,
pleading for us, that we may set forth what cannot be fully
understood."
That is why
those who have experienced
the secret mysteries of God
try to express themselves
by using figures and similes.
If these are not read
with a certain simplicity,
they may seem absurdities,
as in the comparisons
drawn from the Song of Songs
and other books of Holy Scripture.

2.

Therefore, there is no need
to be bound by the explanations given here.
Mystical wisdom, which comes through love,
need not be understood distinctly;
it is given according to each one's capacity of spirit
to accept in faith.
We love God, in faith,
without understanding Him.

I shall deal here
only with the more extraordinary effects of prayer.
There are many writings for beginners,
and you for whom this is being written
have already experienced
the mystical understanding I have spoken of.

I submit all my explanations
to the judgment of the Church
and I wish to explain the more difficult passages
by reference to the Sacred Scriptures.

The Poem:

I.
First steps of the spiritual journey —the longings of
impatient love.

Bride:

Where have you hidden,

Beloved, and left me with my grieving?
You fled like a stag
after wounding me;
I went out calling you,
and you were gone.

Shepherds, you that go
up through the sheepfolds to the hill,
if by chance you see
him whom most I love,
tell him that I am ailing, I suffer, and I die.

Seeking my love
I will pass over the mountains
and the river banks;

I will not gather flowers,
nor fear wild beasts;
I will pass by strong men and frontiers.
O woods and thickets
planted by the hand of my beloved!
O meadow of green pasture,
enameled bright with flowers,
tell me, has he passed by you?

Scattering a thousand graces
he passed by these groves in haste
and looking on them as he went,
with his glance alone
he left them clothed in beauty.

Ah, who will be able to heal me?
End by wholly surrendering yourself!
Do not send me any more messengers;
they cannot tell me what I wish to hear.

All those who are free
keep telling me a thousand graceful things of you.
All wound me more,
and a something I know not
that they are stammering
leaves me dying.

How do you endure,
O life, not living where you live?
the arrows you receive
making you die
from that which you conceive in you of your Beloved?

Why, since you wounded
this heart, did you not heal it?
And, since you stole it from me,
why did you leave it so,
not taking off what you have stolen?

Assuage these griefs of mine,
since no one else can remove them;
and may my eyes behold you,
because you are their light,
and I would open them to you alone.

Reveal your presence
and may the vision of your beauty be my death.
Behold! Love's sickness has no cure
except your very presence and your image.

O Fount so crystal clear,
if on your silvered face
you suddenly would form
those eyes so much desired
which I hold deep designed within my heart!

II.
The spiritual espousal, engagement; preparation for perfect union

Away with them, Beloved,
for I am taking flight.

(The spouse replies):
Bridegroom:
"Come back, my dove;
the wounded stag
appears upon the hill
refreshed in the breeze of your flight."

My Beloved; the mountains,
the lonely wooded valleys,
the strange islands,
the resounding streams,
the whisper of love-laden airs.

The night serene,
the time of rising dawn,
the silent music,
the sounding solitude,
the supper with refreshes and increases love.

Drive off those little foxes,
for our vineyard is now in flower,
while we make a pine-like cluster of roses;
and let no one appear on the hill.

Be still, deadening north wind;
come, south wind. You that waken love,
breathe through my garden;
let its scented fragrance flow,
and the beloved will feed amid the flowers.

You nymphs of Judea,
while among flowers and roses
the amber spreads its perfume,
stay away, there on the outskirts:
desire not to touch our thresholds.

Hide yourself, my love;
turn your face to gaze upon the mountains,
think not to speak;
but look at those companions
going with her through strange islands.

Bridegroom:
Swift-winged birds,
lions, stags, and leaping roes,
mountains, lowlands, and river banks,
waters, winds, and heat of the day
watching errors of the night:

By the pleasant lyres
and the siren's song, I conjure you,
cease your anger
and touch not the wall,
that the bride may sleep secure.

III.
Perfect union; Spiritual Marriage. Longing for the Beatific Vision.

The bride has entered
the sweet garden so much desired,
and she rests to her delight,
reclining her neck
on the gentle arms of her beloved.

Beneath the apple tree
there you were betrothed to me;
there I gave you my hand
and you were raised up again,
where your mother lost her maidenhood.

Bride:
Our flowery bed,
bound with dens of lions,
is hung with purple,
built up in peace,
and crowned with a thousand shields of gold.

Following your footsteps
maidens run along the way;
at the touch of a spark,
the spiced wine,
flowings from the balsam of God.

In the inner wine cellar
I drank of my beloved, and when I went abroad,
through all this valley
I no longer knew anything
and lost the flock which I was following.

There he gave me his breast;
there he taught me a knowledge, very sweet,
and I gave myself to him,
withholding nothing;
there I promised to be his bride.

Now I occupy my soul
and all that I possess in serving him;
I no longer tend the flock,
nor have I any other work
now that I practice love, and that alone.

If, then, I am no longer
seen or found on the common,
you will say that I am lost;
that, wandering love-stricken
I lost my way, and was found.

With flowers and emeralds
gathered on cold mornings
we shall weave garlands
flowering in your love
and bound with one hair of mine.

That single hair of mine
waving on my neck has caught your eye;
you gazed at it upon my neck,
and by it captive you were held
and one of my eyes has wounded you.

When you looked at me
your eyes imprinted your grace in me;
for this you loved me ardently,
and this my eyes deserved -
to adore what they beheld in you.

Despise me not;
for if before you found me dark,
since having looked at me
in me you left your grace and beauty.

Bridegroom:
The small white dove
has returned to the ark with an olive branch,
and now the turtle dove
has found its longed-for mate
by the green river banks.

She lived in solitude
and now in solitude has built her nest;
and in solitude her dear one alone guides her,
who also bears in solitude
the wound of love.

Bride:
Let us rejoice, Beloved,
and let us go forth to behold ourselves in your beauty
to the mountain and to the hill,
to where the pure water flows,
and further let us enter deep into the thicket.

And then we will go on
to the high caverns in the rock
which are so well concealed;
there we shall enter
and taste the fresh juice of the pomegranates.

There you will show me
what my soul has been seeking.
And then you will give me,
you, my life, will give me there
what you gave me on that other day.

The breathing of the air,
the song of the sweet nightingale,
the grove and its living beauty,
in the serene night,
with a flame that consumes and gives no pain.

No one looked at it
nor did Aminadab appear;
the siege was still;
and the cavalry,
at the sight of the waters, descended.

(Taken from **The Spiritual Canticle**, *Saint John of the Cross; Simplified Version with Notes* by John Vernard, OCD.; E.J. Dwyer [Australia] Pty Ltd.

It is the humanity of Jesus that causes us to truly fall in love with God. The following lighthearted meditation is offered as conclusion to this chapter about passionate love with God because in "seeing" the man Jesus, this is where fiery passionate love with God begins.

Snapshots

Come, sit beside me on the couch, and let's look at Jesus' family picture album (as it might have been).

The outside cover of the album has a crown on it with the name lovingly printed in gold calligraphy: "Jesus, Our First Born."

$\mathcal{M}$ary and Joseph are waving goodbye, dressed for traveling; and she looks like she is due any day. And, of course, there is the donkey.

$\mathcal{A}$nna, and Simeon, are both posing with a bundle of blankets in front of a column in the Temple court. Mary is standing beside them with smiling wonder on her face. (Joseph must be taking the picture.)

$\mathcal{T}$here are three dark skinned, elaborately dressed princes or kings kneeling before baby Jesus, who is sitting on His mother's lap, and is being held tightly back. The little chubby hands are reaching for the sparkles almost within His reach, as the jeweled crown is bowed before Him. It looks like He is squealing.

$\mathcal{A}$n Egyptian man is holding three-year-old Jesus up on top of his shoulders, who is going no-handed with abandoned glee. Mary is standing next to them and is looking up at Jesus. It looks like she is telling him to hang on.

$\mathcal{J}$esus looks to be about seven and is holding a medium sized snake, holding it tightly behind its head. He has a rather toothless grin and is holding the snake up to the camera.

$\mathcal{J}$esus is smiling and holding the hand of His step father, Joseph, as the two stand before the main doors of the synagogue. Jesus has a beautiful prayer shawl over His head. It was Jesus' Bar-Mitzvah that day.

$\mathcal{J}$esus, about seventeen, is in a group of other youths; each are holding lambs that had just been sheared. All of them are smiling except Jesus, who has a nervous expression, and is looking over at a lamb, as it is wriggling free from a younger girl's arms.

$\mathcal{T}$his is a picture of a workman's old worn, large-pocketed apron hanging on a hook.

$\mathcal{J}$esus and His cousin are standing in waist-high water smiling at each other in the moment of recognition. Behind Jesus there is a line formed of penitents also waiting to be baptized. It appears Jesus had been standing in line in the water. John, wild in appearance, looks surprised and excited. Jesus is eye to eye with him and looks extremely happy.

$\mathcal{J}$esus is standing at the lectern in the synagogue in Nazareth. He is unrolling a scroll and is smiling, looking down at the scroll in His hands.

$\mathcal{J}$esus is smiling very broadly, and is clinking His wine glass with the bridegroom's at a wedding in Cana. Someone has written the caption below the picture: "L'Chaim!" (To Life!)

$\mathcal{A}$bout a dozen children are dancing in a circle around Jesus, His eyes are raised to heaven and He seems to be shouting in joy.

$\mathcal{J}$esus and Peter are posing on the shore of the lake. Beside them are nets brimming with fish, and men frantically trying to divide them and count them. Peter looks ashen pale and is barely smiling. Jesus has His arm around Peter's shoulder and is smiling broadly.

$\mathcal{A}$ series of pictures are on this page. In the first one, Jesus is standing, looking up, and smiling with a look of amazement on His face. He is inside a dark, crowded room surrounded by listeners packed together, sitting on the floor and filling up standing space. There is a shaft of light going across His uplifted face, from the sun shining through a hole in the ceiling. Dust and chunks of debris are falling all around Him. Jesus' hand is lifted protectively over His head, shielding His eyes as He looks up.

In the next picture there is a stretcher and a man on it being lowered down right in front of Jesus from the hole in the roof. Jesus is laughing, with left arm across His chest and right hand on His chin (a typical thinking position) as He is waiting and watching in amusement. He is standing back a little.

Here Jesus is standing fully in the sunlight flooding in above Him with only the shadows of four heads peering down from above. Jesus is looking up at them and is speaking, with laughter still showing on His face.

Next we see the man who was on the stretcher. He is laughing and dancing, but Jesus is sternly looking at someone across the room, all hints of joy erased from His face.

$\mathcal{J}$esus, Jairus, and Jairus' daughter are posing right outside the beautiful synagogue in Capernaum. Jesus has His left hand on top of the girl's head, and in His right hand is a bouquet of yellow flowers.

$\mathcal{J}$esus and four women are posing and Jesus is holding a child on His hip. It looks like they're camping. Smoke from a cooking fire is behind them. Judas and Matthew are in the background to the right side, waving to the camera.

$\mathcal{T}$his scenic picture looks as if it was taken from a boat on the lake. It is hazy gray. The whole of the picture comprises a very large distant hill, covered with a multitude of people who spread forward to the shore and to its right and left over smaller hills. There is one boat pulled up on the beach.

$\mathcal{J}$esus, the Twelve, and Zacchaeus are all seated together around a low table. Everyone is smiling, and James is pointing to a money bag he is holding up.

$\mathcal{T}$his looks like a frolic in the lake—everyone is splashing water at each other and Jesus, apparently, is getting the worst of it. I wonder who started it?

$\mathcal{T}$his looks like someone sneaked a picture. Jesus is praying, kneeling, His head is lowered, His eyes are closed and He is very serene. There are green leaves around Him, and through branches can be seen water glittering in the sun.

$\mathcal{T}$his is a withered fig tree. A caption written beneath it says, "He cursed it because it was barren. I took this picture of it the next day."

$\mathcal{J}$esus is on a donkey going down a steep hill, coming toward the camera. Many people are waving palm branches. Jesus is waving and smiling.

$\mathcal{T}$his picture is taken at a dinner table. Simon, the healed leper, is on one side of Jesus, and Lazarus, the raised dead man, on the other. They are all smiling.

$\mathcal{T}$his is of the Eastern Gate taken from a higher vantage point on the Mount of Olives. Under the picture is written, "Jesus borrowed Lazarus' camera and took this picture."

There are blank pages ready for more inserts.

A picture of that gate today would show it is bricked shut. Ezek.44:2: "Then He brought me back to the outer gate of the sanctuary which faces towards the east, but it was shut. And the LORD said to me, "This gate shall be shut; it shall not be opened, and no man shall enter by it, because the Lord God of Israel has entered by it; therefore it shall be shut." While the Turks, who built this eastern gate (on top of the original one beneath it) didn't know the real reason why they bricked it shut, God, who knows the beginning from the end knew it would be. With God everything natural has spiritual meaning. That shut-up gate as it stands today says a lot about the spiritual times we're in. Most people still do not recognize our Messiah, Lord. However, though mankind's hearts, in general, have left Him unwelcome, there is a growing number of those who know that we can't block Him out forever. Those who wait for the Bridegroom with longing and eagerness are His bride. They are preparing for His return. He will return when He is finished building His "spiritual" temple. Soon, Jesus will come and there will be a great wedding celebration. He will burst through the blocked gate(s) in a moment. Maranatha!

As the Messiah, the Son of Man, Jesus visited Jerusalem, His symbolic Bride, and passed through her gates with the eagerness and devotion of a true Bridegroom. Being misunderstood and unrecognized was all part of the holy plan for the salvation of His Beloved. He did it all for love.

It won't always be a world under the reign of God's enemies—one day He and His bride shall reign, in love. Eternity and time, earth and heaven, shall be one! Until then we remember, wait and prepare—for the One we've learned to "see."

These last words Jesus said publicly in the temple before He was crucified: "You will not see Me here again until you

learn to say, 'Blessed is He who comes in the name of the Lord.'"
His words were directed to His own Jewish people. These words
will be fulfilled by them. His own, not only His own Jewish people,
but, also, all who belong to God, are coming to see Jesus for
who He really is. Hearts and gates are opening wide for Him—
longing for Him! He is the Desire of the Nations! Soon, He will
come again in the name of the Lord. These are prophetic verses
regarding the coming of the Lord to reign in the New Jerusalem,
from Psalm 24:

>"Lift up your heads, O you gates!
>And be lifted up, you everlasting doors!
>And the King of Glory shall come in. " V. 6:
>"This is Jacob, the generation of those who seek Him.
>Who seek Your face." V. 10:
>"Who is the King of glory?
>The LORD of hosts, He is the King of glory."

Blessed is He—Jesus the Messiah—who comes in the name
of the Lord! The Spirit and the Bride say, "Come."

Prayer Journal Exercises:

1. Spiritual formation is a way we can return love for love to Jesus. Spiritual formation is intentional spiritual disciplines and practices through which we experience our relationship with Jesus—Christian spiritual life. His love comes to us in so many ways. It is up to us to "look" for God and His love in our lives and then respond to Him.

    A life consecrated to God is not all flowery and fun. It is also hard work, suffering, and perservering. We should be progressing to Christian perfection, which simply is: communion and union with God. It calls us to love God with everything we are because He loves us so much. It calls us to die so that we can live in Him. It means that we find our truest identity from God's personal love. The following is a prayer you can make your own.

    > *I give myself to You, O Lord, my maker and most loving God, in humble response to Your great love. It is my desire to live in communion and union with You, wholly consecrated to You, with all my life, forevermore.*

2. Formulate a "rule of life" to keep you spiritually on track. A personal Rule should reflect specific ways to integrate the callings and desires God gives you: how to respond to God by way of spiritual priorities and disciplines for a close relationship with God. The following is an example of a Rule, not necessarily meant to be suggestions:

Sample Rule:

By the grace of God, I intend to:
—Read at least one Scripture every day.
—Pray upon rising and upon retiring for a half an hour each time.
—Go for a 20 minute prayerful walk with the dog, whenever possible, after supper.
—Go away on a personal weekend retreat every summer and fall.
—Attend church every Sabbath, and keep the day as a day of rest.
—Read at least one spiritual classic for every modern book.
—Meet with a spiritual director every two months.
—Serve the poor through some form of charity outreach once a year.
—Meet with a bible study or prayer group, or spiritual formation group once a week every other week.
—Make a new friend in a nursing home and visit once a month.

A person could create a Rule that had daily, monthly, and yearly practices and intentions. A Rule should be as creative as the Creator—and unique to each person. A person's Rule will change as times and seasons change in daily life. One needs to be gentle with oneself. The Rule is to serve the person—not the other way around. It should not be legalistically practiced but should be lived gracefully. God will energize and give desire to follow the Rule, if it is right for that person. Primarily, its purpose is to help form one's spiritual life.

Begin by praying and asking God to help you. Reflect on your life and what you do now. Consider your family situation, job, church involvement, etc. What things should you cut? What would you like to add? How can you fit in personal prayer and journaling, perhaps a class to learn something you've always wanted to learn . . .

this Rule should be based on what you feel God is calling you to be, that you think will be helpful in your relationship with Him and those in your life.

Daily prayer time is essential. All other disciplines should depend upon what God is calling you to be as you determine the correct balance for your "inner" and "outer" life (inner meaning your devotional prayer life and who you are; outer meaning what you do). Prayerfully do this.

These two suggestions are for the serious seeker. The benefits from these two practices can be very significant:

1) Get a spiritual director, a spiritual-friend. Christian spiritual direction is a ministry that has its roots deep in the history of the Church. A spiritual director is one who is prepared through training, experience, and spiritual formation to help another in their spiritual life. A spiritual director is like a mentor who listens and helps in the discernment process regarding one's relationship with God.

2) Go away on a personal, silent, prayer retreat for time alone with God at least one weekend every year.

This is a lot for a prayer exercise and cannot all be done now; however, it is a place to start. Through intentional spiritual formation and devotional habits one will more deeply experience God and spiritual renewal. But keep in mind that God is not as interested in our list of "shoulds" as much as our "loving desire" to know Him. Follow your love to God—your heart knows the way.

Appendix

Recommended Reading List

Once I read a book that gave a suggested reading list at the end. What had shaped the writer of that book became a helpful resource for my own faith journey. This book I've written reflects the writing of many others. I have tried to list those works that inspired and influenced me the most. I hope this list will help you to grow in love for Jesus Christ. ". . . that your love may abound more and more in knowledge and depth of insight. . . . (Phil. 1:9). I am thankful to God and all these writers who wrote to bring God glory.

Classic works on contemplative prayer:

1. Creative Prayer - A Devotional Classic, by E. Herman; Forward Movement Publications; 1985. The author was the wife of a Presbyterian minister and lived from 1875-1923. Creative Prayer is a treasure-packed little book on devotional life. Because of its clarity, depth, simplicity and mystical insights it has become an enduring classic.

2. Experiencing the Depths of Jesus Christ, by Jeanne Guyon; Christian Books Publishing House; 1975. This book was originally published in the 17th Century and was called *Short and Very Easy Method of Prayer* by Jeanne Guyon but was translated from the original French text into modern English, it was retitled in 1975. A powerful influence over the centuries, it contains insights on experiencing Christ which profoundly stirred me. The author herself said about her book, "The purpose of this book is to offer a way in which the Lord Jesus can take full possession of you." If taken to heart, it is a life changing book, no matter where you might be on your faith journey.

3. <u>The Practice of the Presence of God</u>, by Brother Lawrence; Fleming H. Revell Company; 1967. Brother Lawrence teaches about the abiding presence of God in a life of unceasing prayer.

4. <u>The Interior Castle</u>, by Teresa of Avila; translated by Kieran Kavanaugh; and Otilio Rodriguez; ICS Publications, Institute of Carmelite Studies; 1980. A Spanish saint, Teresa of Avila lived in the 1500s. Beset by decades of ill-health, she was asked to write on the subject of prayer by her order's superiors. She uses the "castle" analogy, with rooms ("mansions" the soul moves through) to depict the stages and inner journey of prayer (and of one's spiritual life) to meet the King who abides in the most secure interior room in the castle's "keep" (center). This is a spiritual classic on devotional prayer.

5. <u>The Interior Castle: Saint Teresa of Avila</u>, by John Venard, OCD; E. J. Dwyer Pty. Ltd.; 1988. A simplified, abridged edition of her writings from the original. This is my favorite version. It is divided up by sections according to the seven mansions. Each "mansion" has chapters that describe different spiritual experiences. The chapters are short and the writing style gives the feeling that you are sitting across from Teresa having tea. Even the print layout is in short, poetic lines. About 100 pages, it is similar to a little "reader." Also included is a brief biography of Teresa Avila's life and a concise and informational introduction.

6. <u>The Cloud of Unknowing</u>, author unknown, Image Books/Doubleday, 1973. Believed to have been written in the 1600s, here is one of the most influential works on prayer and spirituality in the history of western Christian spirituality.

7. <u>Dark Night of the Soul</u>, by John of the Cross; Image Books; 1959. John of the Cross, in this historic spiritual classic, describes his experience of God in contemplative

prayer. He was Spanish, and a close friend and colleague of Teresa of Avila. In the 1920s the Catholic church bestowed on him the rare title "Doctor of the Church" because of his depth of spirituality and doctrinal soundness.

Modern Writing:

8. Spiritual Exercises, by St. Ignatius of Loyola. There are many translations and versions of this classic. One which has meant much to me is a workbook called Listening Prayer: A New Annotation and Introduction to the Spiritual Exercises of St. Ignatius. This workbook has been self-published by its author, Jim Wakefield. Organized as a daily devotional, it is broken down into weekly themes. While written from a Protestant perspective, its exercises and meditations are the original ones Ignatius wrote. They focus on the life of Jesus from the Gospels and help bring the reader/prayer into journaling and dialogue with the Lord. They also are a useful introduction to imaginative meditation with a Scriptural basis. To order, write or call: Our Savior's Lutheran Church, 1040 C Avenue, Lake Oswego, OR 97034 - Phone: (503) 635-4563.

9. Too Deep For Words: Rediscovering Lectio Divina, by Thelma Hall, r.c.; Paulist Press; 1988. Lectio Divina is a Latin term for sacred reading, or "Praying the Scriptures." The author's experience as a retreat leader and spiritual director has given her insight and clarity in guiding others in deeper prayer experience. "Lectio Divina was a proven path to contemplation for centuries," says Thelma Hall in the Introduction. Besides her solid traditional Christian teaching, she also provides over 500 Scripture meditation texts by topic.

10. Prayer: Finding the Heart's True Home, Richard J. Foster; Harper Collins; 1992. The most comprehensive book on prayer (all types) and Christian spirituality I've found. A "must read" for all serious students of prayer.

11. The Joy of Listening to God, by Joyce Huggett; Inter Varsity Press; 1986. This book is rich with insights and instruction on contemplative prayer in the course of our busy lives in today's world. She relates her personal experience with candor and honesty. To me, she speaks from God's heart about His desires.

12. Centering Prayer: Renewing an Ancient Christian Prayer Form, by M. Basil Pennington; Doubleday; 1980. A practical teaching on how to experience silent prayer. Joyce Huggett (see above listing) was inspired from this book when she first began her own experience of contemplative prayer.

13. The Way of the Heart, by Henri Nouwen; Ballantine/ Epiphany Books, 1981. This book by one of this century's most influential Christian writers is about solitude, silence and prayer, and how to open our hearts to God's active presence in our lives.

14. Opening to God: A Guide to Prayer, by Thomas H. Green, S.J.; Ave Maria Press; 1977, 1987. This is an excellent introduction to contemplative prayer.

15. The Lover and the Beloved: A Way of Franciscan Prayer, by John Michael Talbot; The Crossroad Publishing Company; 1985. An inspirational and informative book that explains experiences typical for those who enter into a mystical love relationship with Jesus.

16. Heaven Within These Walls: A Spiritual Pilgrimage Out of Disillusionment and Deep Into the Heart of God, by Glandion Carney; Regal Books; 1989. This book includes exhaustive resources for the faith journey. God used this book to confirm my own direction into spiritual formation ministry. It helped me better understand what God was doing in my spiritual life and those around me.

17. <u>How to Keep a Spiritual Journal: A Guide to Journal Keeping for Inner Growth and Personal Discovery</u>, by Ronald Klug; Bantam Books; 1989. A how-to informational book for journal keeping, it covers: benefits, tips, instructions, examples, evaluation guidelines, advice for crafting journal entries, and a lifetime plan for journal keeping.

18. <u>Union Life</u> is a bi-monthly free magazine (supported through free will donations) and is about the incarnational reality/mystery of God in us. It is one of my favorite sources for inspirational reading. Its address: Union Life, P. O. Box 2877, Glen Ellyn IL 60138. Phone: (708) 469-7757.

19. <u>Weavings: "Woven together in love" A Journal of the Christian Spiritual Life</u>. This is a bi-monthly publication by The Upper Room, 1908 Grand Avenue, P. O. Box 189, Nashville, TN 37202. A variety of contributing writers make these booklets contain much to ponder. Filled with poetry, prose, and book reviews, they've added to my library a treasury of inspirational writings I've often shared with others.

Books about Jesus. The following are books that have greatly nurtured my love for Jesus:

20. <u>Divine Romance</u>, by Gene Edwards; Christian Books Publishing House; 1985. An allegorical, imaginatively profound love story about God and His Bride. This work confirmed my faith understanding of God as a our lover.

21. <u>My All For Him</u> by Basilea Schlink; Bethany House Publishers; 1971. Basilea Schlink talks of "first love" for Jesus in this wonderful devotional book. A reader says this in the forward: "As I read this book, my heart yearned to love our Lord more. . . . For Mother Basilea does not merely express the depth of her own love for Jesus. She also shows how we too may ourselves experience it deeply." The author is the foundress of an

evangelical contemplative sisterhood. The order originated in Germany and now has sisters in Israel and the United States.

22. Desiring God: Meditations of a Christian Hedonist, by John Piper; Multnomah Press, 1986. Piper writes about *enjoying* God, the love life we can experience with God and how all areas of our everyday lives are positively effected by it. (The influence of Jonathan Edwards is obvious throughout these pages.) His book gave me a sense of freedom to really enjoy God, which Piper says is the reason were were made. When we live for God alone, and desire God alone, we will be fully satisfied by God alone.

23. The Pursuit of God, by A. W. Tozer; Christian Publications, Inc.; 1982. This book was a catalyst for my desire to see God's face. Reading this was the first time I ever thought of pursuing God for Himself. And, that is where I was at the time in my faith journey. It was a turning point when I left behind loving "what God does" for "who God is."

24. Bible Studies for the Preparation of the Bride: A Study of the Song of Solomon, by Robert Thomas Weiner, Jr. and Rose Ellen Weiner; revised edition 1985; Maranatha Publications (P. O. Box 1799, Gainesville, FL 32601). This is an indepth bible study workbook. It was written for those who are seeking and longing for the Lord Himself. God used this in my life when I needed confirmation that I was, indeed, His bride and that Jesus loved me as a bridegroom loves a bride.

25. Immanuel: Reflections on the Life of Christ, by Michael Card; Thomas Nelson Publishers, 1990. I regard this book as truly poetic (includes meditations for some of his most famous songs). It is an artistic masterpiece of the humanity and divinity of God-with-us. Also a songwriter, Michael Card's music reminds me of David's

psalms and how they might be written today, rich with prophecy and beauty.

26. The Parable of Joy: Reflections on the Wisdom of the Book of John, by Michael Card; Thomas Nelson, Inc., Publishers, 1995. Another joy-filled, wonderful work filled with stories and meditations on the life of Christ and our faith in Him. Very inspiring.

27. God Came Near, by Max Lucado; Multnomah Press; 1987. All of Max Lucado's books are wonderful. One of his first published books, this one is still my favorite because it centers on seeing Jesus. One warning about picking up any one of his books: you could become addicted! When I read his work, I enter into a heart-to-heart encounter with God.

28. The Manger is Empty, by Walter Wangerin; HarperSanFrancisco, Zondervan Publishing House; 1989. Walter Wangerin's books are powerfully inspirational, helping us see Jesus from many wonder-filled perspectives. His artful writing is practical and sublime, while conveying profound insights.

29. Reliving the Passion of Christ, by Walter Wangerin; ZondervanPublishing House; 1992. Through meditations on the suffering death and resurrection of Jesus as recorded in the Gospel of Mark, this one is a poignant book for those seeking a deeper love and appreciation for our Lord.

30. Lord, I Want to Know You by Kay Arthur, Multnomah Press; 1992. Kay Arthur, known for her precept-upon-precept method of biblical study, in this book has written a meditative devotional on the Old Testament names of God—about the character of God. I've used this book in groups and in private devotions. I've been through the study several times and have grown to know God better through it.

31. <u>Everlasting Love: A Story of Love . . . The Kind you've Always Longed For</u>, by Kay Arthur; Harvest House Publishers; 1995. This is a parable story about Jesus and his Bride. The main characters' names are: Joshua and Christianna. Sometimes fiction can best convey truth more than in any other form of writing. This is one. I thoroughly enjoyed this short, engaging story of God's love, faithfulness, generosity, and grace which has encouraged me to wait faithfully and lovingly for my Bridegroom.

32. <u>Three Philosophies of Life: Ecclesiastes: Life as Vanity. Job - Life as Suffering. Song of Songs: Life as Love</u>, by Peter Kreeft; Ignatius Press, 1989. A wonderful book that is inspirational theology at its best! Reading it was a confirming time for me because it articulated and focused many of my own experiences and beliefs. Here is a book that puts truth in a way that you say "Yes!" all the way through it. I especially loved the last section "Song of Songs: Life as Love."

33. <u>The God Who Comes</u>, by Carlo Carretto; Orbis Books, 1974. Carlo Carretto shows how to discern God's presence all around us, and that God's coming to us is continuous. God waits to be recognized in creation, in events, in others, and within oneself. For me, this was an inspiring, comforting and challenging book about how to notice and experience God's presence. Carretto's writing celebrates what it means to know God.

34. <u>The Signature of Jesus: On the Pages of Our Lives</u>, by Brennan Manning; Multnomah Press, 1992. Manning 's books have become fast favorites for many Christians. His books have encouraged me to live radically for Jesus—especially this one. What does it mean to be a true loving disciple and friend to the Lord Jesus? This book really motivated me, gave me things to ponder,

and deepened in me what it means to live in communion and union with Jesus.

35. <u>The Lion and Lamb: The Relentless Tenderness of Jesus</u>, by Brennan Manning; Chosen Books; 1986. Manning meditatively portrays an almost mystical understanding of who God is in this captivating, dramatic writing. "The two aspects of the marvelous character of Jesus: one, His overwhelming power, and two, His gentle kindness wooing you to the love of the Father," is the description on the book cover. I loved this book because it grasped the reality of who Jesus is.

36. <u>Windows of the Soul</u>, by Ken Gire; Zondervan Publishing House; 1996. This book is meditative and written in the true art of spiritual direction—helps one "notice" God in different and new ways. This book itself was a "window" through which my soul did glimpse God—and He was looking at me! It is a book you will want to share with your friends and one you will want to reread. Ken Gire has other meditative books out. <u>Intimate Moments With the Savior</u>; Zondervan; 1989; is another one of my favorites. The meditative, reading experience is very aptly described by its title.

37. <u>Passion for Jesus: Perfecting Extravagant Love for God</u>, by Mike Bickle; Creation House; 1993. This book gets to the heart of the Christian life: intimacy with Jesus. Besides Christian bookstores, it can be ordered through Vineyard Ministries, 800-852-8463.

Credits

Credit for the quotations used in *Love's Face* are as follows, listed in the order of appearance on the given page numbers:

(From the Introduction) *Making Sunday Special* by Karen Mains; republished by Star Song. Used with permission.

Pgs. 49, 50) *The God Who Comes* by Carlo Carretto; published by Paulist Press, c1974. Used with permission.

(Pgs. 50, 51) *Three Philosophies of Life* by Peter Kreeft; published by Ignatius Press, c1989. Used with permission.

(Chapter 6) "The Gardens of the Lord" was inspired by *Divine Romance* by Gene Edwards, published by Christian Books Publishing House, 1985.

(Pg. 103) *Song of Songs* by Watchman Nee, Translated by Elizabeth K. Mei and Daniel Smith; published by Christian Literature Crusade; c1965. Used with permission.

(Pgs. 114-115) *The Lover and the Beloved* by John Michael Talbot; The Crossroad Publishing, c1985 The Little Portion, Inc. Used with permission.

(Pg. 116) *Mystical Passion: The Art of Christian Loving* by William McNamara, published by Amity House.

(Pgs. 116, 118) *Augustine of Hippo: Selected Writings - The Classics of Western Spirituality;* translated and introduction by Mary T. Clark; published by Paulist Press. Used with permission.

(Pg. 119) *Crucified Love: The Practice of Christian Perfection* by Robin Maas, c1991, published by Abingdon Press. Used with permission.

(Pgs. 123-124) *Prayer: Journey from Self to God*; Joann Nesser; 1985, revised and reprinted in 1997; Christos Center for Spiritual Formation, 1212 Holly Drive, Lino Lakes, MN 55038. Used with permission.

(Pgs. 127,128) Prayers/poems from *The Fire of Love*; Penguin Classics; Translated into Modern English with and Introduction by Clifton Wolters, c1972, Penguin Books.)

(Pg. 129) The reflection that begins: *"All deeds are accomplished in passion,"* is from Meister Eckhart, 13th Century. Public Domain. Source unknown.

(Pg. 130) The poem: *Aspirations of the Soul After Christ* by Madame Jeanne Guyon. 16th Century, France. Public Domain. Source unknown.

(Pg. 131) *Divine Love*; author known as "T.P.". A Christian hymn. Public Domain. Source unknown.

(Pgs. 132-133) *Canticle II of The Canticle of the Sun by Francis of Assisi: The Best from All His Works*; *The Christian Classics Collection*; Abridged and edited by Stephen Rost; Thomas Nelson Publishers, c1989.

(Pg. 134) *The Living Flame of Love: Saint John of the Cross*; *Simplified Version with Notes*, John Vernard, OCD; E.J. Dwyer; c1990).

(Pgs. 135-143) *The Spiritual Canticle, Saint John of the Cross; Simplified Version with Notes* by John Vernard, OCD.; E.J. Dwyer Pty Ltd.)

Order Form

Please send _____ copies of *Love's Face* to:

_____
Name

_____
Address

_____
City   State   Zip

Payment:
Send $11.00 check or money order with this tear-out order form
(or equivalent information). Add 6.5% sales tax if sent to a
Minnesota address; add $1.50 for shipping of the first book and
$.50 for each added book.

**Attention church/ministry bookstores and groups, book clubs,
mail order ministries:**
*Discounts can be given for larger orders of the same title to the
same address.*

Send or call in your order to:

LIVING WATERS
PUBLISHING

15590 Highland Av. N.W.
Prior Lake, MN 55372

Toll-free: 888-950-2772   E-mail:
Lvngwtrspb@aol.com